"Aren't you such a cute little girl? You look just like your daddy."

Startled, Cash almost looked around, half expecting to see Isobel's ex, but then he realized the gentleman thought the three of them were a family. Cash stepped farther down the cafeteria line. He liked kids well enough, but had never given much thought to having his own.

"Yep, I do," Lottie responded, clearly not understanding that the older gentleman had assumed Cash was the father. "Daddy got me this necklace with my name on it for my birthday."

She held up the silver chain with her name spelled out in pink crystals.

The man nodded approvingly. "That's a very pretty piece of jewelry. Nice job, Dad."

Isobel sent a grimacing smile Cash's way, her cheeks red with embarrassment. "I'm sor—"

"It's okay," Cash said as he slung an arm around Isobel's shoulders and turned to the man. "I think she looks more like her beautiful mama."

Dear Reader,

Welcome to *A Fairy-Tail Ending*, the launch of a trilogy spin-off of my Top Dog Dude Ranch series!

As a child, I adored fairy tales. (I still do!) But I also could never decide on a favorite. Each of the heroines appealed to me at different seasons of my life. During my more bookworm moments, I imagined myself as Belle. In times of isolation, I identified with Rapunzel. My love of animals reminded me of Snow White in the woods.

In plotting my next three books, I knew I wanted to explore deeper the mystical nature of Moonlight Ridge, Tennessee, home of the Top Dog Dude Ranch. What better way than through fairy tales? Thus, this trilogy was born in my mind as I imagined if Belle, Rapunzel and Snow White were modern-day sisters on a mission. Meet the three Dalton sisters, Isobel (Belle), Zelda (Rapunzel) and Neve (translates to Snow) as they begin their quest in Moonlight, Tennessee, for their grandmother's long-lost child! Their journey starts with Isobel's story in *A Fairy-Tail Ending*.

I enjoy hearing from readers and can be found frequently on Facebook, Instagram and TikTok. Links are on my website: catherinemann.com. Also on my website, check out my latest contest and sign up for my newsletter for the latest scoop!

Happy reading,

Cathy

CatherineMann.com

A FAIRY-TAIL ENDING

CATHERINE MANN

SPECIAL EDITION

Harlequin®
SPECIAL
EDITION™

Recycling programs
for this product may
not exist in your area.

ISBN-13: 978-1-335-40198-4

A Fairy-Tail Ending

Harlequin Enterprises ULC
22 Adelaide St. West, 41st Floor
Toronto, Ontario M5H 4E3, Canada
www.Harlequin.com

Printed in Lithuania

MIX
Paper | Supporting
responsible forestry
FSC® C021394

USA TODAY bestselling author **Catherine Mann** has won numerous awards for her novels, including both a prestigious RITA® Award and an RT Reviewers' Choice Best Book Award. After years of moving around the country bringing up four children, Catherine has settled in her home state of South Carolina, where she's active in animal rescue. For more information, visit her website, catherinemann.com.

Books by Catherine Mann

Harlequin Special Edition

Top Dog Dude Ranch

A Fairy-Tail Ending
Last-Chance Marriage Rescue
The Cowboy's Christmas Retreat
Last Chance on Moonlight Ridge
The Little Matchmaker
The Cowgirl and the Country M.D.
The Lawman's Surprise

Harlequin Desire

Alaskan Oil Barons

The Baby Claim
The Double Deal
The Love Child

Texas Cattleman's Club: Houston

Hot Holiday Rancher

Visit the Author Profile page
at Harlequin.com for more titles.

To my precious sisters, Julie and Beth.
I love you both!

Prologue

Cocoa the Caring Canine

Did you know that dogs can sense magic? Well, it's true.

Enchantment releases a distinctive sugary smell in the air that only our canine olfactory nerves can detect. That aroma is even more enticing than the barbecue in progress next door.

If I'm having an off day with my Labrador nose, luckily real-life fairy tales also release a hum into the air. And I'm guessing you know all about our enhanced hearing since we can detect that doorbell ring even in a deep slumber...

On the second floor...

Burrowed underneath three layers of covers.

Compared to alerting about a ringing doorbell or smoking grill, sensing the musicality and perfume of magic is easy-peasy.

For those of you who are tuning in to my blog for the first time, my name is Cocoa, and I'm all about watching for magic everywhere I go. Somebody has to make sure that not even one note or a single whiff slips by unnoticed.

Unutilized.

Making the most of every magical opportunity is especially important to me because I'm a service dog. A chocolate Labrador retriever, mobility assistance dog to be exact. My whole life is dedicated to the job. Now, don't worry for even a minute about my day being devoted to tasks, because I love to work. I mean really, really love it.

The best day of my entire existence came when the facility where I trained for two years—yes, two whole years—matched me with a forever person to help. Lottie. She's only six, and she uses a wheelchair because she was born with something humans call spina bifida. I can't explain it like a doctor. I just know there's a place in her spine that didn't close up right when she was inside her mom.

So I help Lottie. I go to school with her and pick things up, like her pencils, when she drops them. I push elevator buttons with my paws—I like putting extra oomph into that cue. I lay over her lap and press if she's having nerve pain—or if she's sad. Don't we all need a hug every now and then? I can even pull the covers up for her with my mouth.

How cool is that?

When Lottie's asleep, sometimes I help her mama—Isobel—when she is sad. Usually when she curls up in her reading chair, those tears start leaking. I'm not sure if it's because she's tired or worried about Lottie or sad that Lottie's dad doesn't live with them. The reason doesn't matter to me. I'm all about the solution that I offer best. More of those special hugs that are designed to press just right.

But lately, I'm worried I may not have enough cues up my sleeve to give this family. The last time I went with Lottie to the doctor, things got a lot more complicated. She needs all the magic I can sniff out. The doctor says she needs a new kidney.

My sniffer also tells me she needs it sooner than they think.

Chapter One

Who wouldn't be charmed by a man who dressed up as a swashbuckler for a child's sixth birthday party? And as a single mom, Isobel Dalton certainly wasn't immune.

Besides, she figured she was due a bit of covert drooling over the firefighter wearing an eye patch and red head scarf while folding himself into a tiny chair for a tea party. Her friend had gone above and beyond today.

Cash Warner, aka charming pirate guy, lifted his little pink cup in a toast. "Ahoy, matey!"

"Yo-ho-ho!" her daughter Lottie echoed, dark pigtails sticking out from under her paper pirate hat.

The rest of the children at the other tables followed with a jumbled chorus of "Surrender the booty" and "Shiver me timbers!"

Isobel pressed a hand to her mouth to hold back a laugh, thankful for the happy distraction from the upcoming reading of her grandmother's will. Gran. Her rock. Gone for one month.

But Gran would have been the first to insist this birthday be celebrated. Lottie had requested a pirate tea party, and somehow the plan had come together. The logistics had been a challenge, because this celebration wasn't hosted at a park or in a family backyard. This kiddie get-together was being held in the activity room of a physical therapy rehabilitation clinic where her daughter received both physical and occupational therapy for the effects of spina bifida.

Lottie had invited children she'd bonded with over the years at the center. Like her best friend Jasper, who carried a different superhero lunchbox each week. A premature delivery had left him with cerebral palsy. And newcomer Isla, who'd lost a leg in a car accident, but given how quickly she was adapting to the prosthetic, she was spending less time inside these four walls.

Isobel adjusted the pirate scarf around her head, easing her ponytail back over her shoulder. She and Lottie had spent endless hours a week here since her daughter was born with the condition that affected her spinal cord. Some of them were painful hours. Others more uplifting and liberating. She would never gain full use of her legs, but thanks to her service dog Cocoa and the staff here, Lottie increased her independence daily.

Medical equipment beeped and shooshed lowly in the background. Undisturbed, the chocolate lab rested beside the wheelchair with her head on her paws, immobile but ever ready for a task. Staff were positioned throughout the commons area, albeit wearing party hats to match the children's. Chicken nuggets were labeled "cannonballs," and fruit skewers were held together by miniature plastic swords. Placemats resembled treasure maps for a hunt that would take place at the end. The sheet cake was decorated like an ocean and sported a chocolate ship on top. A treasure chest overflowed with party favors…

And no matter how much Isobel looked around the room, her gaze continued to land on the muscular firefighter giving Captain Jack Sparrow a run for his money.

"What did the ocean say to the pirate?" he asked, a parrot puppet on his hand.

Lottie's arm shot up. "Nothing. It just waved."

"That's absolutely right, matey." He passed a mesh bag of candy doubloons into her eager hands.

Cash had come to the rehab center about six months ago after being injured on the job battling a housefire. He'd rescued five of the six family members before a falling beam had shattered a leg and an arm. His journey to recovery had been difficult. And not only from the broken bones and the painful skin grafts over his burns. She could tell the memories still haunted him, even if he refused to speak about that time in more than cursory statements.

Although no one would guess at the moment. "How much does it cost for a pirate to get his ears pierced? A buck an ear."

Silence met that joke. The pun seemed to have flown right over their heads.

"Get it?" he explained, tugging each ear that sported a clip-on gold hoop. "A buck…an…ear. 'Buccaneer' is another name for 'pirate.'"

Realization spread over each little face until giggles

erupted, mixed with exaggerated boos from Jasper at the corny joke.

Lottie waggled her fingers again, looking too cute for words in her costume—a vest and sash with loose black-and-white striped pants. "I got one. Wanna hear?"

Cash tipped a salute in her direction. "Go for it."

"Where does a pirate put his trash?" She only paused for a minute as if rushing to make sure no one else got to say the punchline she'd been practicing all morning. "In a garrrrrbage bag."

At the laughs from the rest of the children at the clinic, Lottie beamed, rocking from side to side in her chair until her napkin slithered to the floor.

Cocoa promptly plucked it up, the paper trailing like a checkered flag from her mouth, and dropped it back onto Lottie's lap. Lottie plucked a dog treat from the pouch clipped to her waist.

With an all-in drive for her job, Cocoa thrived on picking up everything from a dropped pencil to a favorite doll. Cocoa could even tug on socks. Sure, Isobel could help with these tasks. She was Lottie's mom, after all. But her daughter battled for every bit of independence, so much already having been taken from her. Cocoa's aid gave Lottie that freedom.

A priceless gift.

On her best days, her daughter could maneuver with the assistance of a walker and leg braces. Others? Lottie needed her wheelchair. And always by her side, good and bad days, her service dog Cocoa.

Who also happened to be the "voice" of Isobel's newest blog. Her freelance writing allowed her flexibility to be present for all the appointments, a benefit she did not take for granted. Especially since her ex-husband spent so much time on the road as a truck driver. And they desperately needed his insurance.

Since her divorce and reclaiming her maiden name, her life in Montana has been filled with work and her daughter Lottie—until a surprise friendship developed between her and Cash over lunch in the cafeteria. He'd sat next to her one afternoon when the place had been packed, then the next day even though there had been empty seats available. A pattern began.

A pattern she would miss deeply now that his recovery was drawing to a close. She was glad for him. Truly.

He certainly looked fit and ready to return to work.

Her shoulder was jostled by Jasper's mom as she angled nearer to whisper, "Cash is yummy, don't you agree?"

Isobel glanced over quickly. Could the woman be interested? Isobel's stomach flipped, then settled as she remembered that the young mother was happily married to an art teacher who'd given Lottie an assortment of the drawing supplies, along with the promise of lessons.

"Of course I agree," Isobel said. There was no denying the obvious.

"Then what's stopping you from making a move?" Anna elbowed her. "You're single. He's single… I think?"

From the other side, another mom, Evelyn, an executive who always brought a full briefcase, added, "He most certainly is. I did a deep dive on his social media, and he's single." She winked. "I was only checking for my niece, of course."

The full-time father across from her laughed. "Make sure you get his number before these ladies scoop him up for their single relatives."

Heat crawled over Isobel's cheeks, but she knew insisting she had no room for a relationship would make no difference to determined, well-meaning matchmakers. So she settled for a more benign answer. "Thanks, but we're just friends."

Good friends.

Friends who spent weekends hanging out together.

Evelyn snorted. "What kind of magic do you wield that makes a *friend* dress up for a kids' birthday party? Because I would pay good money to get my husband in that getup. And not for a kiddie party, if you know what I mean."

Isobel shrugged. How could she explain the simple truth? "He's a great guy, no question."

Cash's friendship had been a godsend to her over the past six months. She looked forward to their dinners together after rehab sessions. Movie outings. Having a plus-one for a big rodeo fundraiser for the clinic. And now he was restored to health. He would be moving on with his life, and she wanted that for him even as nerves made her ill with impending dread of the first time she would pull up in the parking lot knowing that he wasn't inside.

She knew their relationship would never be more than friendship. Her bruised heart couldn't handle more. But she was lonely. Her marriage had been lonely. Life after her divorce wasn't any different.

Her ex-husband loved Lottie and tried his best to spend time with her. Except he traveled for work so very much, and his job as a truck driver brought in decent money. And with Lottie's medical bills they definitely needed every extra penny. Her career as a blogger was taking off, particularly her "Cocoa the Caring Canine" writings, keeping her all the busier. Which didn't leave much time for a social life.

Cash's friendship these past months had been a sanity saver.

A friendship she could no longer afford to even fantasize about taking further, as Cash would soon be moving to another fire station far from her. Today, she needed to focus on her child and getting through the Zoom call with the attorney about her grandmother's will. An impending conversation that made her eyes sting already.

But she would face that as she faced every day now. Strong and alone.

For the past six months, Cash Warner had counted down the days until he could say goodbye to this rehab clinic, put the pain behind him and reclaim his old life.

Except, now that the time approached, his gut knotted with something he couldn't name. Something that insisted he wasn't ready to put this place in his rearview mirror and reenter the work world. But there wasn't a choice. He was finished here and would return to his job in three weeks, relocating to a new department on the other side of the state.

He would say goodbye not only to this place but to Isobel and Lottie…and of course Cocoa. The knot in his gut twisted tighter.

In the clinic courtyard, Cash shoved aside the unease. He'd offered to keep Lottie and Cocoa occupied while Isobel cleaned away the party mayhem.

He scooped up the tennis ball and tossed it for the chocolate Labrador retriever. Cocoa sprinted ahead, past a fountain, leapt and snagged the ball out of the air on its first bounce. The leggy canine trotted over to Lottie in her wheelchair under the concrete water fountain.

Giggling, the little girl plucked the toy from her lab. "Good, Cocoa. Now go get it."

Lottie tossed the ball into a bush, and the dog sprang into action again, pouncing and foraging. They could keep this up all day serving the dual purpose of exercising her service dog and increasing Lottie's arm strength. Cash had learned that every task here at the clinic had a purpose, pushing toward independence.

Man, he was going to miss this little girl and her mom.

At least he'd gotten to help with the party today, a small thanks for the way their friendship had saved his sanity as he'd recovered from the injuries in the five-alarm fire. His wounds were minor compared to what his fellow firefighter, his best friend Elijah, had suffered. Elijah had lingered for five days before dying from the burns that covered eighty percent of his body.

Even thinking about it filled Cash's senses with that awful scent of smoke…and his friend.

He swept his bandana off his head and stuffed it into his back pocket. "Did you get everything you wanted for your birthday, kiddo?"

"Everything. And a lot more." Pitch. Wait. Beyond the low brick wall, cars rumbled in and out of the parking lot. "It was the best party ever. Thanks bunches and bunches for all the new toys for Cocoa. And I really like the matching collar and T-shirt you got for Cocoa and me. But most of all, thanks for being a pirate. That made Mommy really happy too."

"My pleasure, kiddo." He shot a quick glance over to the picture window showcasing the moms and dads helping Isobel clean up and load gifts. Isobel bustled at the speed of light, her trim legs in yoga pants and an overlong T-shirt with a pirate dog image. She had a scarf tied around her head, swashbuckler style, big hoop earrings glinted, and her thick ponytail trailed over her shoulder stopping just shy of her—

Nope. Not going there. He tore his gaze away. He'd offered to help, and she'd asked him to keep Lottie entertained for just a few minutes—easy enough. "Glad I was still around to attend."

Pitch. Wait. "Will we get to see you now that you're better?"

"Of course, but when I go back to work, they're sending me to a new fire station in a new city."

Lottie chewed her bottom lip. "Oh, right. Mommy told me. I kinda hoped she was wrong. We got firemen here too, you know. But I guess now that you can run and stuff, you'll want to do things with your old friends."

"Hey," he knelt in front of her. "I love playing ball with you and Cocoa. But I also have to pay my bills, which means going where the job sends me."

For as long as he could remember, he'd wanted to be a firefighter. Every Halloween growing up, he wore variations of the same theme. His family hadn't had much money, so the costumes had been homemade from clothes around the house. A two-liter soda bottle had been repurposed into an oxygen tank on his back. Another year he'd carried a big red cardboard fire hydrant, and his dad wore a paper bag house with crimson tissue paper flames. Another year he'd made a fire engine out of an old box. He'd colored every inch of it in great detail for weeks leading up to October 31. He'd been crushed when it started raining and the box fell apart.

But as much as he yearned to be back on the job making a difference, he would miss Isobel, Lottie and Cocoa. The counselor—mandatory after an accident like the one he'd suffered on the job—had asked if they represented the security of the rehab facility.

He'd bristled then, still did. He wasn't *afraid* to go back to work. In fact, he owed it to his partner, who had died in that accident, who hadn't gotten a second chance like him. But Cash hadn't been ready to delve into the reasons why he wasn't ready to leave the rehab center—not for the counselor and not even for himself.

Lottie dropped the tennis ball beside her footrests. Cocoa huffed and flopped onto the ground beside it, drawing Cash's gaze over to Lottie's furrowed face. "Aw, kiddo, no need to look so sad. Is there something else wrong? Are you not feeling good? Maybe too much cake?"

She shook her head. "*I'm* okay."

"Are you sure?" He dragged a lounge chair over and sat in front of her, searching her wide blue eyes. "You look sad, way too sad for a birthday girl."

She picked at the loose black-and-white striped pants. "I'm just worried about my mommy."

"Your mom?" Concern nipped at him. He thought about Isobel setting up the party, now cleaning up, on top of all the time she spent writing. She looked tired. Overworked maybe? People assumed she had it easy working from home as a blogger, but he knew the long hours she put in to make a success of her "Cocoa the Caring Canine" brand. "What's going on?"

Spring sun beaming down around her, Lottie leaned closer and whispered, "She was crying this morning. She tried to pretend like she wasn't, but I saw her wipe her eyes and her nose with a tissue."

Crying? Now that wasn't like Isobel at all, and it tore him up to hear as much. As far as he'd seen, she was the eternal optimist. "You're a sweet kid to care about your mom. Hopefully it wasn't anything big." He made a mental note to let her know her kid was concerned while, at the same time, trying to keep Lottie's worries at bay until her mother could address them. "My mom cries at the drop of a hat."

Her eyebrows pinched together. "What does that mean? Drop of a hat?"

Lottie conversed with adults so easily, sometimes he forgot to speak in simpler terms. "It means that she cries easily. Like as easily and fast as a hat falling to the floor."

"That's a silly thing to say." Lottie scrunched her nose. "Why not say she cries as easily as I forget to brush my teeth?"

"That a really good question." And a really good way of phrasing things. Maybe the kid was destined to be a writer like her mother.

"Besides, my mommy doesn't cry when a hat falls or when I forget to brush my teeth." She tugged the end of one of her braids, a self-soothing habit of hers he'd noticed. "I overheard her tell my daddy she has to be strong 'cause of all my doctor visits. That made me sad."

His heart squeezed in his chest. This kid sure got to him. "I'm sorry you overheard something like that."

"So when I saw my mommy crying this morning, I knew it had to be very bad. Can you help her?"

He wanted to. Very much. But he didn't have a clue where to start. "I think you need to talk to your mom about it. It's not good to keep your feelings bottled up… Uhm, by bottled up, I mean keep them all inside."

"Oh. Do you let yours out?"

Was the kid listening in on his counseling session? Because her admonition sure sounded like Dr. Thomas 101. "I thought we were talking about your mom?"

"Can you help her?"

"I intend to try." When had he been able to say no to this cute kid? That's what landed him in a pirate costume at a tea party. He grinned, imagining the grief he would get over those photos if Elijah saw—

His chest went tight and a roar started in his ears. When would he stop looking for his friend around every corner?

Cash cleared his throat. "What do you say we get some water for Cocoa?"

Lottie nodded. "And while she's drinking, I can wipe the slobber off the tennis ball. Yuck."

She wiped her palms on her pants.

The dark cloud over his mood edged away a bit. Lottie had that knack. Great kid. But children weren't in the cards for him. Since his breakup, he was committed only to his career. Dangers on the job had put too much stress on his relationship. His girlfriend had left. She hadn't even issued an ultimatum. She'd vowed she loved him too much to ask him to give up the profession he lived for. He'd offered to give it up anyway. She'd insisted he would resent her. And she left. That was it. No tears or shouting. Just complete silence.

His gaze darted back to the picture window view of Isobel, her hair swishing as she loaded gifts into a wagon. Her face was tipped to the other parents, and she smiled at something. Even from a distance, he knew instantly how her bluish-green eyes would sparkle and that a husky laugh would follow.

He remembered well the first time he noticed both. She was reading a romance novel, amused by one thing or another. He never knew what, only that he couldn't look away from her. He stared for so long that she looked up over the top of her page and her gaze held his. Just as he started to apologize, her smile went wider and she'd plucked another book from her bag and offered it to him. Unable to resist, he'd taken it, read it from cover to cover, trading it for another the next time he'd seen her.

Everything about Isobel then and now was full of light. Yes, he enjoyed basking in the glow she brought, even to the simplest tasks like adding sprinkles to a milkshake or watching a sunset. But he had a wealth of darkness in him, not just from the divorce. The accident haunted him.

And he refused to add one more weight to Isobel's already complicated life.

Chapter Two

Dragging a packed and heavy wagon full of party gear behind her, Isobel thumbed her car key fob, a beep sounding just before the back hatch of her mini-van raised. The bright Montana sun made everything in the sparsely populated lot glisten with the promise of summer, later than the southern weather she was used to having grown up in North Carolina, but all the more welcome for the wait. Normally, that was just the recipe to brighten her mood.

Today? It only made the throbbing behind her eyes stronger until she longed to climb under the covers for a two-day nap. She wished she could attribute the ache to too much computer time, but she knew it had more to do with the stress of the upcoming call she couldn't avoid.

The sooner she packed away the party gear and bags of dog food the kids had donated for a local shelter, the sooner she could get the conversation over with. Thankfully, the donations had also given her an idea for a blog about the food drive. Thanks to the posts she'd been including from Cocoa's point of view, she'd seen a significant uptick in followers and advertisers.

Isobel hefted up a forty-pound bag and slid it into

the back of her minivan. The upcoming Zoom appointment to discuss her grandmother's will weighed on her, squeezing her heart with guilt over not being there for Gran in North Carolina during her final days. How had she and her sisters become so distant too, when once they'd been so close to each other, especially during those summers at Gran's? Tears burned her eyes over so much loss.

"Let me help you with that," Cash's voice warmed her an instant before he leaned into her line of sight to swing up the next bag of kibble on top of the other already in back. "You've already had quite a workout today."

"I'm stronger than I look." A by-product of lifting Lottie and her wheelchair. "Are you sure you should be picking those up yet?"

He quirked an eyebrow. "You wound me, lady. But rest assured, I've been cleared by the doctors. I'll be returning to duty in three weeks. Those sacks of feed are a lot lighter than carrying a person over my shoulder."

"Then I'll accept the help gratefully while I stash away the gifts."

His smile made her breath hitch somewhere in her chest until she saw sparks from lightheadedness. But she couldn't stop herself from tracking his long-legged movements.

He eased his backpack to the ground, the red kerchief hanging out. With each move from the wagon to the vehicle, he limped ever so slightly. At times, she could almost forget what he'd been through except for a scar on his forehead from an ember that left a red patch about two inches long. His pirate costume of black pants and long-sleeved shirt covered the scars on his leg and arm. But she recalled them well from months of seeing him in workout clothes.

No doubt, he'd come a long way in six months with a determination that she admired. And he'd done it alone every step of the way. No visitors. Not even once. She'd tried asking him about his family and friends from work only to have him change the subject.

Cash slung the last of the bags into the van, stowing the collapsible wagon, and pressed the Close button. But he didn't leave. Sighing, he pressed a hand against the back window, his deep brown eyes focused on her. "I need to ask you something, but I don't want to be presumptuous..."

Isobel winced. "Way to tee up that statement."

"Yeah, you're right." He thumbed the scar on his forehead absently. "That didn't come out well, so I'll get straight to the point. Lottie told me she's worried about you because she saw you crying this morning."

She sagged back against the van, feeling like a failure. She'd tried so hard to make this day perfect for Lottie, and yet she'd still let her own baggage steal some of the joy. "My grandmother passed away a month ago."

"Ah, man," his hand fell from his forehead to rest on her elbow. He squeezed lightly. "I'm sorry for your loss."

The warm calluses along his fingertips more than comforted her, tempting her with the gentle abrasion of each subtle caress. Easing back a step, she hugged herself. "I hate that Lottie saw me in that shape. I thought I was past the initial wave of grief."

"You're human," he said softly. "And you simply showed your child it's okay to be upset sometimes."

She gave him a wobbly smile. "It's just all fresh again because I heard from the lawyer today about settling her estate. She left a letter for me in her will—actually a letter for my two sisters as well." She shook her head, the band on her loose ponytail slipping even lower, strands swinging free along her cheeks. "I don't mean to ramble on."

"I asked because I care about the answer," he said, sincerity ringing through.

"Thank you." She tucked a lock of hair behind her ear only to have it slide free again. She was a mess today on all levels. "You've already been such a great friend. I don't mean to unload on you."

She yanked the ponytail band free and slid it onto her wrist, shaking her hair free around her shoulders. Was it her imagination or had his eyes lingered? On her? Her mouth went dry.

Then he was scuffing his gym shoe along the pavement, staring at the ground. "You've seen me during some of my most embarrassing moments. Remember that time I was so proud of myself for doing a half-hour circuit on the rehab equipment only to find out I had a rip in the back of my gym shorts."

She laughed, the sound almost clearing the tears clogging her throat. "You wore tie-dyed boxers."

"You did drop that glass of water to distract people

from staring at me, but it was too late. I appreciated the effort though."

"Aww, it was nothing." Her smile tipped higher. Her eyes met his, held, her heart pounding in her ears. "Well, the meeting with the lawyer is in thirty minutes."

He raised his hands. "Then I won't keep you from leaving. You're barely going to make it home in time."

"Actually, it's via Zoom. With my sisters too." She hitched her computer bag over her shoulder. "I'm going to buy Lottie a milkshake in the cafeteria to keep her occupied while I find a quiet corner to take the call." Luckily, the clinic had strong public Wi-Fi.

He tipped his head to the side toward the meditation garden with concrete tables and soothing water fountains. "You can take your call at a table over there. I'll keep Lottie and Cocoa entertained. We had a blast there while you packed up the party gear." He added with a wink, "I'll take the milkshake as payment."

As much as she worried about taking advantage, she was too weary to say no. Cash and his tempting broad shoulders would be gone from her life soon enough. "Thank you."

Once Cash said goodbye to this place, he would miss Isobel, Lottie and some of the staff, even though they'd put him through intense pain at times. But he absolutely wouldn't miss the cafeteria food.

The rehab cafeteria was small, but at least they rotated choices of baked blah, broiled blah and grilled blah. So the families of long-term patients weren't stuck eating the same thing again and again. Sorta. Along one wall, glassed refrigerator units housed juices, salads and premade sub sandwiches, the space's saving grace.

He'd shared many a meal and milkshake here with Isobel and her daughter and looked forward to this one as well, making the most of the time they had left. As he walked toward the counter lining the back wall, the clang of silverware against dishes and conversation echoed louder than normal in the open area. The intercom interrupted thoughts with calls for staff and announcements of special events. Low music would have been nice, but he had yet to hear so much as piped tunes here or in the elevators. A mystery, because some soothing music would have gone a long way toward bringing a little bit of Zen to a stressful place.

Stepping into line, he waited until Isobel and Lottie approached. Now was not the time to check out the sway of Isobel's hips. She needed his help, not his interest.

Weaving around tables, Isobel exhaled hard, huffing her bangs off her forehead. "Thanks for holding our place." She shot an apologetic look to the people behind him. "We just had to make a quick pit stop in the ladies' room."

Lottie wheeled her own chair, navigating the line, with Cocoa keeping perfect pace beside. "Do they still have any chocolate shakes? They always run out of that flavor first."

Cash grinned. "We're in luck. There's even vanilla for your mom."

Lottie clapped. "They need some strawberry milkshake fans, 'cause it seems like they always have plenty of that flavor left over."

In front of them, an older gentleman using a walker to maneuver after his knee replacement surgery paused, grinning. "Aren't you such a cute little girl? You look just like your daddy."

Startled, Cash almost looked around, half expecting to see Isobel's ex, but then he realized the gentleman thought the three of them were a family. Cash stepped farther down the cafeteria line. He liked kids well enough, but he'd never given much thought to having his own—yet another subject his counselor probed relentlessly.

"Yep, I do," Lottie responded, clearly not understanding that the woman had assumed Cash was the father. "Daddy got me this necklace with my name on it for my birthday."

Lottie held up the silver chain with her name spelled out in pink crystals.

The man nodded approvingly. "That's a very pretty piece of jewelry. Nice job, Dad."

Isobel sent a grimacing smile Cash's way, her cheeks red with embarrassment. "I'm sor—"

He waved aside her worry. "It's okay." He slung an arm around her shoulders and turned to the man in the knee brace. "I think she looks more like her beautiful mama."

Isobel's cheeks went pinker and she stuttered, "Uh, th-thanks."

And she was pretty, very much so with her dark hair falling loose around her shoulders now. Her hoop earrings tangled in the locks as if inviting him to smooth them back.

Yes, pretty. But clearly tired.

There was a lot in his life he couldn't fix, but this he could address. "I'll carry our food." He added three shakes to the tray, along with straws and extra napkins. "We can sit way over there under that willow tree. It's close enough to the swings that you can still see Lottie, and you'll be in the shade for your call."

"That sounds perfect…" She hitched her laptop bag more securely onto her shoulder. "I could have managed, but it's nice to have your help."

"My pleasure, ma'am."

She smoothed a hand over Lottie's hair, tightening the pigtails. "We're going to miss seeing you here, but I'm so thankful you've recovered."

An itchiness welled inside him that he couldn't explain, not to the counselor or even to himself. He only knew the sensation crept in whenever he thought about returning to work. Which made no sense, because he wanted to regain his previous life.

He loved his job as a firefighter, even the twenty-four hour shifts at the station that others claimed put too much pressure on the homelife. But he was okay with that. He didn't want roots. "I'm gonna miss both of you, a lot, and these milkshakes as well."

And the confounding thing about it? He wasn't lying.

Isobel tipped the screen of her laptop to diminish the sun's glare peeking through the weeping willow. Which also gave her a better view of Cash and Lottie.

Focus. She needed to focus.

She hadn't seen her sisters since Gran's funeral last month, and before that, it had been nearly two years since a sister get-together. Gran had been sad about that, no matter how much Isobel tried to explain that they were all just mired in day-to-day business.

Isobel balancing work and Lottie's care.

Zelda working double shifts in a dog-grooming salon and volunteering at a local shelter in her remaining free time.

Neve establishing her career as a college professor, mired in paperwork.

Adulting was hard.

More and more, Isobel felt rootless. Yes, she had Lottie, but what kind of extended family would she be able to offer her child? She wanted her daughter to have memories like she did, growing up with grandparents and siblings. But she didn't feel capable of managing that alone, and trusting a man again felt daunting if not impossible.

And there was no older generation to spoil Lottie. Not just because Gran was gone. Her ex was estranged from his parents. And her parents had died in a car accident less than two months after the youngest—Zelda—graduated from high school. They'd had such plans for empty-nesting. Travel. Redecorate. Reconnect with old friends. Even cooking classes.

Tragically, the tickets for their celebratory cruise went unused.

Gran's grief had been tangible over losing her only child. Isobel and her sisters had taken turns visiting her, trying to fill her days with distraction. Dividing and conquering had seemed the best plan then—it still did. But it also led to more distance, a disconnectedness between the three of them.

There'd been a time she was close to her sisters, but not so much anymore. Life had sent them in different directions. Isobel to Montana. Zelda to Georgia. And Neve relocating within their home state of North Carolina. She hated that for herself and for Lottie.

The computer screen flickered to life with one boxed image: Zelda. Then another, Neve. What a sad kind of family reunion, nothing more than some cyber waves connecting them. They all three had their grandmother's dark hair and bluish-green eyes, but their personal tastes kept them from looking identical.

Seeing Neve and Zelda's faces now, Isobel realized just how much she'd missed them. Sister time. The silly and playful. And, yes, Isobel wouldn't have minded having the emotional support of family. She saw it with others at the facility and couldn't help but be envious of the shared laughs and tears, that connection of history and collective experiences that made words unnecessary at the times of deepest stress.

Neve seesawed a pen on her desk, diplomas littering the wall behind her in her college office. "This could have all been accomplished with a certified letter."

The middle child, Neve had always been a nature-loving academic, a free-spirited hippie. She seemed happiest in the woods searching for herbs and making necklaces out of flowers. No one had been surprised when she took a job in the Biology Department at Appalachian State University.

Zelda toyed with the end of her coffee-brown braid. "Gran always did have a flair for the dramatic."

Youngest of the sisters, Zelda was a dog groomer, a city girl who lived in Atlanta. Not that Zelda was out partying, in spite of her chic looks. Her boyfriend was the controlling type who'd alienated most of the family. Isobel had tried to reconnect, but her sister had cut her off. A hurtful—and worrisome—reaction. Isobel still didn't know how to bridge the gap.

Neve's pen paused midtap. "Flair for the dramatic? Or she was being bossy. Like you, Zel."

Isobel rushed to keep the peace. Old patterns were hard to break. "If it brought her some joy to think about us on this call together, it's the least we can do for her. In honor of those summers spent with her."

"You're right." Neve nodded with a sigh. "I get it. There's no need to pile on the guilt."

Zelda crinkled her nose. "And there's no need for you to be so cynical."

Gritting her teeth, Isobel gripped the edge of the concrete table, at a loss for how to defuse their bickering. At least Cash was watching Lottie, so she could focus on the meeting.

The screen flickered with the addition of a fourth face—thank goodness for the interruption—the attorney, Silas Green. Silas had been Gran's next-door neighbor and companion for many town outings. Seeing his familiar face brought back memories of North Carolina summer picnics with pimento cheese sandwiches and lemonade before swimming in a nearby river. For a long while, Isobel had wondered if they were a couple, but nothing had ever come of it. Gran had always insisted her heart was already taken.

Silas tugged lightly on his goatee, his law office behind him like a higher-end version of Neve's college office. Diplomas sporting more mats and gold tipped frames. "You know your grandmother was a dear and cherished friend. I miss Alice every day when I go out to get my mail and she's not sitting there on her porch with her morning cup of coffee and a book."

Isobel's grip tightened on the table until the concrete bit into her palms. "Thank you for being there with her at the end, Silas." Gran's heart attack had happened out of the blue. She'd updated her will before going into surgery but didn't survive the procedure. None of them made it in time to hold her hand and say farewell. "You were special to her as well."

"Alice Franklin Dalton was a complicated woman." He angled forward, arms on his desk by a brass scales of justice knickknack. "There are things about her past that she didn't share with many people."

Zelda dropped the end of her braid. "What do you mean?"

"How much do you know about Moonlight Ridge, Tennessee?" Silas asked.

Isobel's grip eased on the table, and she folded her hands in lap. Her grandmother had made up fairy tales that focused on that region, but Gran's family was all from North Carolina. "Oh, you mean her stories? She certainly had a way with spinning a magical tale."

Their father had also been brought up on Gran's fairy tales, so much so, in her honor, he'd insisted on each of his daughters having an enchanted name. Iso-*bel*, in reference to Belle from *Beauty and the Beast*. Zelda, a nod to Rapun*zel*. And Neve, a French word for the first snow, a more obscure reference to Snow White.

Oftentimes, Isobel wondered if those names had steered their destiny in some kind of self-fulfilling prophecy.

The attorney quirked a bushy eyebrow. "Moonlight Ridge is more than a fairy-tale location. It's a real town, small, nestled in the Smoky Mountains. It was virtually unknown until a few years ago when a young couple started a dude ranch located there. You may have heard about the Top Dog Dude Ranch."

Shaking her head, Neve frowned. "Never heard of it. And I'm not sure what a dude ranch has to do with Gran."

"Bear with me." Silas lifted an arthritic hand. "While she was growing up in Moonlight Ridge, your grand-mother met the love of her life there as a teenager."

The love of her life? Isobel scratched her chin. "But Gran didn't meet Gramps until her twenties…"

Which meant that she'd fallen for someone else long before then? If so, why hadn't she told anyone? Gran had never been one to hold back.

Or so they'd all thought.

"That's right," Silas continued, his eyes compassion-ate in a way that hinted there was far more to come. "She loved someone before your grandfather and it didn't work out. What's more, your grandmother had a baby with this man. The child was given up for adoption."

Neve gasped. "A baby we don't know about? Gran's baby…our uncle or aunt?"

Zelda waved her hands with agitation, costume jewelry on her wrists and fingers glittering. "I'm gonna need a minute."

Isobel let the revelation sink in for a moment before asking, "A boy or a girl?"

Not that it mattered, but it was a place to start picking through the mountain of questions piling up in her mind.

"A son," Silas answered.

Isobel worked to wrap her mind around this shift in her universe. Of course Gran had been entitled to her privacy, to her secrets. But hadn't she understood the practical implications of this more recently? They'd known for about six months that Lottie might need a kidney transplant someday. No one on either side of the family was a match, and there had been no luck in finding a nonrelated match either.

Having additional relatives to reach out to, this son and whatever children he may have had offered a hope beyond measure for Lottie, who already faced such monumental health struggles. And Isobel didn't intend to waste a moment of time focusing on frustration over not hearing sooner. "Silas, do you know where this man is now?"

"I'm afraid I don't," he said apologetically. "But your gran had a final wish that the three of you would find her son and give him the crystal ring that her first love gave her all those years ago."

The crystal ring, a beautiful amber gem in an antique gold setting. One that Gran had always put on when she told her fairy tales, insisting it had magical powers to create fantasy worlds.

"Us? Find him?" Neve leaned back in her office chair, skepticism stamped all over her face. "Aren't there agencies for that?"

"Well," Silas continued, easing the knot on his necktie, "it's complicated since the courthouse caught on fire, destroying records from that time period that indicate the organization—or private party attorney—who would have handled the placement. Alice was young then, and her father handled the legal work. You may need to get an investigator, and of course, you can look into matters for yourself. Regardless of the route you choose, Alice insisted that Moonlight Ridge is the place to start. She left enough money for the three of you to stay at the dude ranch there for the summer...longer even, if needed."

This all sounded far-fetched, even for Gran. If it weren't for Lottie's situation, Isobel would turn the whole matter over to a private detective without batting an eye. But she couldn't afford to pass up the least opportunity to expand the donor base since she, her sisters and her ex-husband weren't a match.

Zelda worried her bottom lip. "And what if we say no, Silas?"

"It's what your grandmother wanted. When she updated her will just before surgery, she was under the impression it was possible for you each to take the summer off—if she didn't survive."

That sure quieted the conversation. Isobel reached for her water bottle to wash down the lump in her throat, one that grew at the thought of Gran spending her final time on earth thinking through pain and regrets. Would she have torn up that will if she'd lived? They would never know. All she could do now was focus on Silas's words.

"As I understand it, you, Neve—" he held up one finger "—have a research sabbatical this summer. And Zelda—" two fingers "—works a temp job that she can leave at any time. Here's a want-ad listing for a dog groomer at the Top Dog Dude Ranch. And Isobel—" three fingers "—your freelance writing career gives you total flexibility."

Already Zelda chewed on a thumbnail. "I'm still not sold on this. I vote for the private detective idea."

Absolutely, they should hire a professional. But Isobel didn't intend to simply pass over this search to someone else and twiddle her thumbs while she waited. She would make this journey on her own if necessary, but having her sisters' help could speed things up, and time mattered more than ever for Lottie. She'd never asked her family for help. Not once. Lottie was *her* daughter, and she wanted to be the one caring for her. But now? This?

Family needed to stick together and she would do whatever it took to get them on board. "If we find him, he might be a donor match for a new kidney for Lottie. Please."

Neve's mouth dropped open and Zelda blinked in comprehension, both silent for two heartbeats, which felt like an eternity. Why hadn't they made the connection right away like she had? Were they that distanced? Isobel prepared herself for disappointment.

Finally, Neve smiled. "Of course. I'm there for you and Lottie."

Zelda's grin was shakier but her voice resolute. "Count me in."

Isobel gripped the table again, this time in intense relief, to keep herself from toppling over off her seat.

Silas smiled, his hand gravitating to his goatee. "The timing of this is almost magical, don't you think? Your grandmother couldn't have planned it better."

Chapter Three

Worry was chewing Cash alive one tennis ball toss at a time. Time passed, picnic tables being vacated one after the other as patients returned to their therapies and staff resumed their workday.

Finally, though, it appeared her call was drawing to a close. Would she confide in him? Given past experience, he expected she would, and that nipped him with guilt when he thought of all he hadn't shared about himself.

While Lottie turned her attention to a video game, Cash stuffed the dog's toys into the canvas bag while Cocoa kept her post by the little girl. He wasn't able to hear what was said to Isobel since she used earbuds and kept her voice low. But she'd run through the gamut of emotions. Shock. Hope. Frustration. Back to hope.

What in the world had they been talking about? He prayed it was positive news. Maybe her grandmother left a surprise fortune that could make Isobel's life easier. Not likely, but worth hoping for.

As the sun sank lower in the late afternoon, she kept her head tucked down as she tucked away her laptop and slid from the concrete table under the willow tree.

With each step she took closing the distance between them, he could see her sliding walls up to shield her exhaustion and stress.

Had she always done that? If so, why hadn't he noticed before?

An overbright smile on her face, Isobel dropped onto a flat swing nearby. Lottie was still engrossed with the video game on her new tablet—a birthday gift—and Cash took the opportunity to talk to Isobel uninterrupted.

He braced his hand on the swing set frame. "Are you okay? You look like you've seen a ghost."

"My grandmother's ghost," she said darkly before shaking her head. "I'm sorry. That wasn't funny. I'm just a little bit…well, in shock, I guess. The lawyer shared some major bombshells."

"The good kind, I hope?" he prompted, seeing a glint in her eyes. "The equivalent of a lottery win?"

"Better." She gave him a tearful smile. "Apparently my grandmother had a secret love child, a son, when she was a teenager. She gave him up for adoption. She wants us to locate him."

The import hit him—hard. It was almost too good to be true. "Lottie. A possible kidney donor."

She toed the swing into gentle motion before continuing. "I'm afraid to get my hopes up. Who knows if he's even still alive?"

"Expectation management is easier said than done." He was an expert on the pitfalls of that. "There's always the chance he's got extended family who could also be tested."

Eyes closed, she inhaled deeply, traffic rumbling in

the distance. "That would be amazing. Sometime I'm going to have to wrap my brain around the fact that Gran had this whole other past that we never knew about. Later though. Right now, I'm focused on Lottie's health."

He drew her up and against his chest, holding her close and doing his best to ignore the softness of her curves, the scent of her flowery shampoo. He exhaled hard and stepped back. "Any clue where you're supposed to start searching?"

Her lashes swept up, her blue-green eyes meeting his. "The will indicates we should start looking where the story began—Moonlight Ridge, Tennessee." She grimaced. "It's in the Smoky Mountains."

"The mountains?" Uh-oh. He'd learned a lot about her over the past months. "You get vertigo on the merry-go-round. No offense intended, but I know your aversion to heights."

After the spring thaw, he'd suggested they celebrate his return to driving with a trip to a state park. Reluctantly, she'd agreed, then spent most of the car ride along scenic mountain roads with her face buried in a pillow. No wonder she lived in a valley.

Even now, her face paled at the mere mention of the elevation. But her jaw was set. "For Lottie, I would brave Space Mountain. Without a seat belt."

Of course she would.

"It's one of the things I admire most about you." He'd been drawn to her caring heart from the start—she wore those emotions in her eyes. "You're an incredible mother."

She blushed, as if she wasn't used to compliments. And this one was on such an obvious subject. Why didn't the people in her life let her know her worth?

Not that he'd seen much in the way of family gathered around her to praise her. She always had excuses for their absence... Her sisters lived in their home state of Georgia. Her ex traveled for work—following him to Montana when they were married had seemed like a good idea at the time.

Isobel sat on the swing again, her foot tapping restlessly. "Gran left enough money for my sisters and me to spend the summer at some dude ranch located there. She wants us to take the time to find her son and return the promise ring her boyfriend gave her."

"That's kinda cool." From everything he'd heard about her grandmother, the woman seemed to value family above all else. Apparently, that had rubbed off. Isobel was the most dedicated mother he'd known.

"It is. Very cool. I know she worried about all of us growing apart, so no doubt this is meant to draw us together." She picked at her pirate scarf belt. "I just wished she'd told us sooner. I don't understand how she could have missed the importance of this news for Lottie."

He wasn't sure what to say to that.

She raised a hand to stop him. "I'm not looking for answers. I'm thankful for the now. And I'll just get plenty of refills on my vertigo medication."

In that moment, he knew exactly what he needed to do with his remaining time off before returning to work. He was a man of action who couldn't afford to second-guess himself on the job. A moment's hesitation could—had—cost him so much.

It cost his friend everything.

Cash gripped the swing's chain, bringing her to a halt. Then kneeling in front of her, he clasped both her hands. "Let me help you. I can drive you to Tennessee."

She looked at him like he'd grown another nose. "It's something like seventeen hundred miles from here. I looked it up while we were on the call. I couldn't possibly impose on you for something like that."

"I'm done with rehab, but I have three more weeks of recovery time before I start the new job." In a new town, away from all the memories of that last fire. "I'll be going stir crazy. You'll be doing me a favor."

"I don't know about that."

"Well, I do." He scratched the back of his neck, along the thin ridges of scar tissue. He'd let his hair grow longer to cover it. "It's not good for me to be alone with my thoughts about the accident."

"You know I'm here if you ever need to talk." She rested soft fingers on his, stopping just shy of the scarring. He'd worn his hair shorter back then, and some had been shaved for treatments. She would have seen it all.

"Thanks." He stopped scratching to link hands with her, squeezing gently before letting go. "I'm still processing. But who knows, maybe sometime in that drive along the mountain roads, maybe I'll be ready to open up."

She tapped him in the middle of his chest. "You're just trying to make me feel less guilty—although that's sweet."

"Say yes." He closed his fist around her touch, clasping stronger this time and holding her eyes with his.

She hesitated for so long he starting lining up arguments in his head to persuade her, even though he wasn't sure why this was so important to him. He knew one thing for certain.

He wasn't giving up.

A long sigh shuddered through her as she leaned into his hold ever so slightly. "Yes. And thank you. I don't know how I can ever repay you."

And he didn't know how he could ever explain to her all the ways she'd helped save his sanity over the past months. That would necessitate explaining just how close he'd been to giving up, a confidence he wasn't comfortable sharing with anyone still on this earth. Not even Isobel.

"You can find that long-lost child and every relative until we get a donor for Lottie."

Only four more hours of driving until they reached Moonlight Ridge, Tennessee, and Isobel could take her face out of the pillow. But as much as she wanted to power through the rest of the trip to end the torture of mountain driving, Lottie needed to stop and Cocoa needed to stretch her legs.

A rest-stop picnic was in order.

Isobel snuck a peek at Cash in the driver's seat as he steered her van onto the off ramp. He'd been a pillar of strength while packing and driving. His offer had taken her by surprise, but he'd been insistent. Heels dug in deep. And she'd been too overwhelmed by the huge life transition to argue for long.

Now, the Smoky Mountains soared ahead of them, a mix of rock walls and lush forest. Beautiful. But so. Very. High. She owed Cash more than she could ever repay him for all his help.

The past five days had been a blur of activity from packing to move to researching a medical network for Lottie in Moonlight Ridge, a town so small and remote that most of her care would take place in nearby Gatlinburg. She'd sublet her Montana apartment and packed the basics, which turned out to be enough to fill a small trailer with the necessary toys, clothes, medical supplies and so much more.

She'd considered flying and simply shipping her gear—for all of about ten minutes. She needed her van.

Yet another reason to be eternally grateful that Cash had offered to drive with her. The thought of tackling mountain roads while towing a trailer would have been beyond bearing and he'd been so effective in making his case.

After mapping out the trip, they'd decided to break the trip into two days, sharing the driving—and sleeping in separate hotel rooms. She and Cash had struck a deal. She would drive on the flat stretches. And when they reached a mountainous leg of the journey? She would be beyond happy to bury her head in a pillow.

At the end of his time in Moonlight Ridge, he would fly home. Without them.

But she didn't want to think about saying goodbye

to him. Better to focus on the present and the picnic lunch ahead of them.

Cash parked the van and trailer longways to avoid backing up. "All right, ladies, let's unload."

With a synergy they'd perfected over the past two days, he unbuckled Cocoa and took her for a quick walk to water a tree while Isobel transferred Lottie into her wheelchair. The rest area was sparsely populated, and in half the normal time—thanks again to Cash—they were seated at the picnic table, with Cocoa snoozing underneath.

Isobel flipped open the wicker picnic basket. "Today's meal is much simpler than yesterday." To save money, she'd cleared out the last of her pantry for meals on the road and at the hotel. The perishables had been gobbled up on the first day. "Today we're finishing off PBJs, apples and chips. Plus a jar of pickles."

She worried too much about Lottie's medical bills and the impending kidney transplant to waste anything. Even a half-eaten jar of gherkins.

"This is awesome. The jam tastes homemade." He folded half a sandwich into his mouth like a starving man.

"It is," Lottie exclaimed, plucking up a section of her sandwich. Crust cut off. Quartered. "From when we went strawberry picking on a school field trip. Mama, can I watch a cartoon on my tablet while you talk to Cash?"

Normally she would say no, not at the table and point out she could do that in the car. But these were special circumstances, and they still had hours left to travel before they reached their final destination. The sunshine and fresh air would be refreshing for all of them.

Isobel tucked a water jug onto the table. "Of course. Vacation rules are different from home rules. But be sure to keep a watch on Cocoa's water bowl. Let me know if it runs low. It's warm today."

"Yes, Mama. And I'll eat all my lunch." Lottie tucked her earbuds in and scooped a glob of peanut butter off a spoon with an apple slice.

Isobel angled closer to Cash. "I don't want you to think I'm asking too much of her." She poured a handful of chips onto a paper towel. "Of course I'm watching Cocoa's water and food, but I also need to help Lottie form positive habits in caring for her service dog."

"You're a good mother. I would never question your rules." He stole a chip from her pile. "Actually, I've learned a lot about service dogs from Cocoa. And about the dedication of keeping her training tight—dedication from Lottie and from you."

"It's worth it for the freedom she offers my daughter." She twisted open another water bottle. "But enough talk of serious things. Let's enjoy lunch."

"You don't have to tell me twice. Your refrigerator cleanout is impressive."

"I'm particularly proud of the dessert—the trail mix that combines all the leftover dried fruits, nuts and three half-eaten bags of candy."

"Hmmm," he hummed as he picked out the M&M's and Sour Patch Kids.

"You're a big kid." She laughed, biting into her sandwich.

"Guilty as charged." He scooped up a handful of the trail mix. "Did you get any more information about your grandmother's childhood?"

The lawyer had provided precious little in the way of direction other than a contact at the local library. As best she could decipher tracking by Gran's maiden name, Alice Franklin hadn't spent all of her growing-up years in North Carolina, only moving there for college, where she met the man she married—Isobel's grandfather—and thus she changed her name to Alice Franklin Dalton. "Just the address of the house where she lived during her teen years and where she went to high school. I spoke with a librarian who told me there are some records in the basement that haven't been scanned into the public database yet."

"How long until your sisters arrive?"

What would they think of Cash? And the fact that he'd accompanied her? She hadn't told them, and now that almost seemed to make a bigger deal out of his presence. "Zelda will be arriving first. If she's on schedule, she'll be there before us. Neve had some last-minute details to take care of at the university, but she should arrive a couple of days after us. It makes my head spin how quickly things have played out."

"The timing sure seemed to line right up for you all to leave for an extended period. It's like your grandmother orchestrated some kind of divine intervention."

That certainly made more sense than magic. "Neve had already given notice on her lease. Originally, she'd planned to tour the state parks in a camper during her sabbatical."

"A real back-to-nature gal." During summers with Gran, Neve had always been the one to collect frogs in a bucket so she could compare their markings and note the details in her journal. Of course, Neve then set all the frogs free, leaving crickets and earthworms nearby for them to snack on as thanks.

"Pretty much. Zelda went to her landlord and begged out of her lease. Luckily, Atlanta is a hot market. She'll only have to eat a month's worth of rent."

"And she was okay with that?" he asked with an arched eyebrow.

"She seemed quite eager to get away." Isobel hadn't given it much thought at the time, but now, she wondered over Zelda's insistence her boyfriend wouldn't be coming along...

"Well, a summer at a resort, all expenses paid, is enticing."

He was probably right.

She shook off errant thoughts and focused on Cash's generosity in helping her drive. "I hope you get some R and R before your flight out, because otherwise, I'm going to feel even more guilty for taking advantage of you this way."

He dusted chip crumbs from his hands. "I looked up some details on the Top Dog Dude Ranch, and it sure has a lot to offer. Not just horseback riding. But whitewater rafting." His brown eyes lit with excitement. "Backpacking. They even have an outdoor theater with a smoothed-out part on the mountain face for the screen."

"None of that was there when my grandmother grew

up in the area. Just the tiny town of Moonlight Ridge and the Sulis Cave. Apparently, it has healing springs inside that flow into a river."

Cash scrubbed a hand along the back of his neck. "I could have used that six months ago."

"You've come a long way in a short time." In those early days of his treatment, he'd been so racked with pain, she wasn't sure he'd even realized she was there.

He'd been zeroed in on making it through each day. She suspected he hadn't been taking his full doses of pain meds either.

"It didn't feel short to me," he said with a dry laugh.

"I was—am—impressed all the same." She closed a hand over his. "I'm glad you have your life back."

The connection lasted an instant too long, their eyes holding before he shrugged aside the compliment. "Lottie is always the impressive one. Whenever I felt like throwing in the towel, I would catch a glimpse of her in PT. She's a tough cookie." He glanced toward Lottie, who was giggling at her video, a hand draped over the side of her chair to stroke Cocoa. "The dude ranch is a wonderfully ADA compliant facility. No worries about wheelchair ramps, bathrooms or widths of doors. There's even an equine therapy camp with adaptive saddles. She's going to have a great summer."

"I hope so." She had researched programs like theirs and always found them too expensive. "This is more than I could have offered her at home. The camp for children with disabilities is one the best I've seen, and trust me, I've looked into quite a few."

"You're both going to be busy."

"I will have my sisters' help."

"And mine for at least a couple of weeks."

Their eyes met and held again. He chewed slowly, his throat moving in a long swallow. He had one of those broad necks—the football player kind. Or firefighter. A person of strength and physicality.

She'd noticed before, of course, but the awareness ramped to a new level the farther they drove from Montana. This was new territory for them on a lot of levels, but she wasn't prepared to think about that now. He'd be leaving in two weeks, so that constant hum of attraction didn't bear thinking about.

"Lottie," she called, her voice squeaky. "Time for us to load up and get back on the road."

"But, Mom, Cocoa isn't ready."

Standing, Isobel gathered the trash—napkins, plastic bags, water bottles. "Well, sometimes life doesn't give us many choices, kiddo."

And didn't she know that. This moment being a case in point.

It might be his leg of the trip to drive, but she wasn't going to do much sleeping, no matter how mountainous the road. Her senses were buzzing, her nerve endings all on high alert just from too much eye contact with this man. She would just sit in the back with Lottie and Cocoa, her focus on typing out her next blog. Her writing and her child's well-being were her life.

She didn't have the bandwidth—mental or emotional—for anything more.

Cocoa the Caring Canine

Time passes in a different way for dogs than for people. We pooches live more in the moment. And right now, it feels like this trip to Moonlight Ridge, Tennessee, is never, ever going to end. I like car rides, don't get me wrong, but my butt has made a permanent dent in the back seat of this van as I log the miles beside Lottie.

More than anything, I want to stick my head out of an open car window and let all those notes of magic fill my nose, my ears flapping so I can hear the music. Even with the window up, the smells and tunes are coming through the vent, and I'll have to settle for that. I can tell, though, that the magical perfume is growing stronger with every mile.

How many more miles though? Tough to tell.

Since—did I mention?—they still won't roll down the window!

It's not like I could jump out if they put the window down. My people keep me in a seat belt harness that's clipped to a special hook. They used to latch it to the seat belt receiver, but I know how to work that. One push with my paw and—bingo—I'm free. I don't know why they're surprised. I use my paws and nose for far more complicated tasks. I can even open the dryer door and put everything in a basket. The laundry part is one of my favorites because it's something I can do that always makes those happy endorphins radiate from Isobel.

Today, though, the happy endorphins are muted by stress. I'm all about sticking close to Lottie because new places are tougher for her. Counters are higher in stores. Ramps leading inside aren't always level or even in good condition.

This van is so thick with emotions, it's a wonder I can smell anything.

Isobel is nervous.

Cash is worried.

But I can't concern myself with the two of them. There's only one of me and Lottie is my girl. She comes first for me. I guess Cash and Isobel are just going to have to help each other.

Chapter Four

By the time Zelda Dalton crossed the Tennessee state line, she had to pull over and breathe through a panic attack. Not that she had a problem with heights like her sister. Her stress came from a different source, one that she'd left behind in Georgia.

She leaned her butt against the front quarter panel of her vintage Volkswagen convertible, bending over to grip her knees as she sucked in sweet breaths of air. From the front seat, her dog Maisey yipped, a senior Maltese.

"Do you need a break, girl?" Zelda rasped. "Because I sure do."

Maisey tipped her head to the side, yellow bows on her ears bobbing. She dropped into a pretty sit, her version of nope. If Maisey needed out, her paws would be digging in the seat. Zelda sighed. How ironic that she read her dog better than she understood some humans.

Straightening, Zelda pushed away from the car and back behind the wheel. "All right, Maisey, time to hit the road again."

The sooner she got there, the sooner she could quit looking over her shoulder. Maisey curled up into a ball on the front seat as Zelda slid the car into first gear. She revved the engine and steered along the winding road, following the posted signs giving directions, wooden and painted pawprints.

The Tennessee mountains were dressed in spring green, a shade more in the teal family that would soon deepen to summer hues. A much-needed soothing tableau. She'd always considered herself an upbeat tough-as-nails person. But leaving Atlanta had been harder than anyone would ever know. Tougher than she could admit, because the truth was so painful.

She'd tangled her life up with the wrong kind of man.

In the beginning, Colin had been so charming, every dream come true. Then slowly, he'd changed, isolating her from her family and friends, cutting her down with small insults. When she'd broken things off with him nearly a year ago, she'd thought she could reclaim her life right away. But it was as if he still had an invisible hold over her until leaving her safe world filled her with panic.

She had managed to extricate herself from the relationship but still felt like a shell of herself. A fraction of the woman she'd once been. She ate, slept, and went to work at the pet-grooming salon. The only time she felt remotely alive? When she volunteered at the animal shelter giving dogs a makeover.

In one of her most desperate moments, she'd met Maisey volunteering. Maisey's previous owners had suddenly developed allergies—after having the dog for nine years. Not-so-coincidentally, their "allergies" had started right about the time they heard about an impending move.

Zelda had taken one look at the heartbroken, overgrown pooch and scooped her up, stinky fur and all. She hadn't regretted the decision for an instant. "We're almost there, Maisey-mine. You're going to love it here. I promise."

Was she trying to convince the dog or herself?

It didn't matter either way, because her sister and her niece needed her. Gran wanted this. And Zelda wouldn't let them down. She would push through, one grounding breath at a time. Hopefully the temp groomer's job at the Top Dog Dude Ranch would keep her too busy to think about the mess of a life she'd left behind. Or too busy to think about how uncomfortable she felt about leaving Atlanta in the first place.

She nailed the accelerator and rolled down her window—her hand pumping the handle on her 1976 Bug. Wind tunneled through the mountain peaks, carrying crisp air into the valley where the Top Dog Dude Ranch was situated. She navigated up the winding mountain path. Towering pines grew around deep-set ancient boulders, the trees scenting the air with summer.

Her cell phone rang, saving her from compounding worries. The caller ID scrolled a call from her sister… Neve. They talked regularly, but how had she let so much time pass between their last visit?

Yet another way she'd allowed Colin to narrow her life. She stabbed the Answer button to connect the call.

"How much longer until you get here? There's something wrong in the universe when I'm the first one to arrive." Zelda usually got sidetracked by any number of things, from losing her keys to talking to helping strangers find a stray dog.

"As soon as I can get out of here. Two days. Three tops."

"That sounds like a cop-out to me." Finally, she passed through the arched entry to the dude ranch, the wooden plaque painted with dogs inside a border of horseshoes. The tree-lined road widened into a clearing with the main lodge, stately, like a rustic castle nestled in the foothills of towering mountains.

"You're the one who doesn't pick up her phone when I call you." Neve's pointed comment needled at her, a covert way of searching out answers for Zelda's behavior for the past year.

But she didn't have a clue how to share the emptiness she felt. The fears. Any of it.

"I'm talking to you now." Deeper and deeper she drove along the two-lane road leading toward the main lodge and little town square. Shops clustered around the sprawling building—a gift shop, Bone Appétit Café.

"But before—is something wrong?" Neve had always been the intuitive one.

The last thing Zelda needed was anyone rooting around in her head. She had enough trouble deciphering her thoughts without added input from a well-meaning relative.

"It's all good," Zelda said quickly. "See you soon."

She thumbed the Disconnect button before her sister could argue. Maybe it was a good thing she'd arrived here first. She would have time to settle in and get her bearings.

Get a grip on herself.

After passing the lodge, she punched the accelerator, downshifting up an incline toward the private cabins nestled into the mountainside. She'd already checked in online, so she only needed to follow the digital map to where…

Three small log cottages perched in a row on their own private path, surrounded by pines. The individual accommodations had been paid for with money left by Gran. Thank goodness they wouldn't be under the same roof. She loved her sisters, but she valued her privacy.

Each sported a small firepit with Adirondack chairs and was encircled by a picket fence, the cabin name spelled out on a plaque nailed to the gate. Solar lights lined the walkways along with bright, floral landscaping. All were utterly inviting and a world away from her condo in Atlanta.

All the better.

The first cabin had a wheelchair ramp, so she assumed that one was for Isobel and Lottie. No vehicle was parked outside, but according to their text exchange this morning, she expected them to arrive by the end of the day. That left two more cabins. She chose the last in the lineup since it was more isolated.

Although, the ranch offered more privacy than she would have expected. Sure, the website made it look spread out, but she'd figured that was just marketing. She'd envisioned a resort, with the cabins all packed in close to the main lodge.

This was a little slice of pastoral paradise.

She turned off the engine and lifted the parking

brake, sagging back in her seat. "Well, Maisey, we're home—for as long as that may be."

Long enough to help her niece.

And long enough for Colin to finally move on so she could hit the reset on her life.

She scooped up Maisey and flung open the door, a light rumble vibrating the earth under her feet. Surely they didn't have earthquakes here?

Wouldn't that be just her luck?

The sound of horse hooves echoed, growing closer, giving her a moment's warning before a palomino nosed through the forest, ridden by a cowboy about fifty feet away. At least she assumed he was. A Stetson was tipped low over his eyes, shading his face from view.

A vacationer?

Or an employee?

Either way, her pastoral paradise had been invaded.

She had no time for anyone except her family and her animal clients. So unless the cowboy had a shaggy pooch, their paths would not be crossing.

Cradling her Maltese, she made fast tracks for her cabin, trotting up the steps and stopping at the door to punch in the security code from the confirmation email. She tapped the lock once.

Twice.

A third time.

The lock blared red repeatedly.

She slumped back against the porch post. Maisey swiveled her head from Zelda to the door, then back again. "I know. I'm trying."

No doubt she'd jammed up the whole thing, like using

a password too many times, then navigating a contorted process of verifying identity.

"Do you need some help?"

A voice rumbled over her senses, vibrating the air around her as tangibly as those hoofbeats had shaken the earth. Sighing, she closed her eyes for a moment before turning to the witness to her embarrassment.

Yep.

The tall, dark and cocky cowboy.

She hated the defensiveness—worse yet, the insecurity—that seared through her until her ears rung. She hated the self-doubt, a reminder that Colin still had a hold over her, even from a distance. It wasn't this stranger's fault she couldn't work the stupid door lock.

But she also wasn't going to give the code to a stranger. Which meant she would have to get back into her car and go to the main lodge for assistance.

She braced her shoulders and forced a smile. "Thanks for the offer, but we're okay. Right, Maisey?"

He stared at her for so long she thought for a moment that he would press the point.

Then he tipped his Stetson and clicked his horse into motion. "Have a nice day, ma'am."

As she cradled her dog to her chest and ran to the safety of her car, she couldn't escape the truth racing after her. She wasn't okay. Not at all.

Carrying a suitcase in each hand and a bag over his shoulder, Cash angled sideways through the cabin's front door and booted the wooden panel closed behind him. "This is the last of the gear from the minivan. Would you like me to unload the trailer now or in the morning?"

He sidestepped the pile of cases, then wove past the dog sniffing every corner while Lottie wheeled around the great room. The late-day sun slanted through the part in the plaid curtains, lending a warm glow to the log walls.

Isobel pivoted from the kitchen counter to face him, open cabinets behind her revealing shelves already stocked with food. "Wow, you're done already? Thank you. I hope it wasn't too much for you, with your leg and all?"

"All good," he reassured her before restating, "and the trailer?"

"Let's wait until tomorrow. We have everything we need in the suitcases, and I'd really like to make it to the welcome ceremony this evening. Not that we're lacking for food."

He nodded. "Looks like they've thought of everything."

She closed the cabinets and strode toward the refrigerator, her socked feet silent against the tile floor. "But if you'd rather rest and enjoy the quiet, I'm completely okay with taking Lottie and Cocoa on my own."

"I wouldn't miss it," he said, adding the newest batch of luggage to the rest, finally free to look around the space as Isobel went back to taking inventory of the food.

Truth be told, he was grateful for the reprieve from the minivan after hours spent in close proximity to a woman who tempted him far too much. He hoped the time at the Top Dog Dude Ranch would give him some fresh perspective on moving forward with his life. A shot at some healing for his mind and soul, since they were both lagging far behind the pink scar tissue that covered his burns.

If the rustic beauty of this place was anything to go by, the rest of his time at the ranch would be a vacation to remember. A stone fireplace stretched to the high ceiling, an antler chandelier sprawling overhead. Log walls, pine and leather furniture rounded out the decor. But more than that, he took in details he never would have noticed before his accident.

The doors were wider to accommodate a wheelchair, perfect as Lottie explored, her squeals of delight echoing to the rafters. The kitchen counter was lower in places where Lottie could roll right up without having to reach awkwardly. The bathrooms sported rails and an accessible shower. And the list went on and on. Such simple—and crucial—additions that could make or break a trip for Lottie.

The excitement on her face lit up the space as she explored the living room. "Mama, what do all of those signs say?"

Cash hitched his thumbs in his back pocket. "They're signs about being positive, but each one relates to dogs."

"What about that one?" Lottie pointed toward the fireplace, a massive piece of driftwood over the mantel with painted lettering.

"Stay paws-itive," he read, before motioning toward another over the archway framing the hall. "Anything is paws-ible."

Lottie giggled. "I can read that one." She gestured to a plaque on a stand beside the sofa. "I love you fur-ever."

Cash applauded. "Well done."

Pun and all.

Lottie beamed proudly. "You taught me that kind of bad joke with those pirate riddles."

Isobel glanced over from the refrigerator. "You're a quick study."

"Can I explore some more, Mommy?"

"Of course," Isobel smiled.

"Come on, Cocoa," Lottie called.

Cocoa's head popped up and she trotted alongside. Doggy nails clicked on the wood floor, and Lottie rolled her chair down the hallway an instant before her squeals echoed. "Look at my room! There's a stuffed dog on my bed. There's even a cowgirl hat on my pillow. Yeehaw!"

Isobel clapped a hand over her mouth. Cash couldn't stop his low chuckle, their laughter tangling up in that way of a long-term friendship. Except lately, it hadn't felt so simple.

He cleared his throat and dropped to sit on the sofa. "Did you find out where your sister Zelda went? I thought she beat us here. Didn't I see her car outside? But she didn't come out."

"She texted." Isobel sank onto the second sofa across from him, swinging her feet up to rest on the coffee table. "Zelda got locked out of her cabin and went to the main office for help. Then decided to stop by the grooming salon while she was out… That's Zelda. She'll find her way over eventually."

Was she hurt that her sister wasn't waiting? It seemed strange that Zelda was so blasé about seeing Isobel and Lottie after so long. But then what did he know about sibling relationships.

"I realize the ranch is new, but somehow this place is just like the stories Gran told us when we spent summers with her. I thought they were fairy tales. Little did I know…"

"You spent the whole school break with her?"

"Every year," she nodded. "Our parents worked summer jobs teaching abroad. Gran had a farm—a small property, not worth a lot except in sentimental value."

"The most valuable currency." Like the costumes his father used to make for him, all the more treasured for the memories made. "So that's where you get your storytelling skills."

Her smile lit her bluish-green eyes until they sparkled like jewels. "Whether you know it or not, you just paid me the highest of compliments."

"Easy enough for me to do." He pressed on, determined to pay her more of those kudos she deserved and yet received so few. "You're very talented. 'Cocoa the Caring Canine' has quite the following."

"I just chronicle Cocoa's day." Grinning, Isobel wriggled her toes in her pale pink socks. "She's the real talent."

It was more than that and he knew it. Isobel's aptitude, her business acumen and her tireless hard work. The afternoon in the rehab courtyard where she'd spent half an hour of her lunch break snapping photos of the dog and Lottie while they played, careful to focus solely on the service animal since she didn't share her child's image online. Countless times in rehab, he could see the dark circles under her eyes that testified to the late hours she spent at the computer after her child went to bed.

He was in awe of her.

The click of Cocoa's nails signaled her and Lottie's return just before they entered the great room.

Lottie wore her new pink cowgirl hat with pride. "Hey, Cash? If 'anything is paw-sible' at the Top Dog Dude Ranch, does that mean I'm gonna get my kidney?"

The child's words stopped him short. He didn't have a clue how to answer. What was the balance between hope and reality when dealing with such a little child facing a mammoth battle?

He looked to Isobel, hoping she saw the plea in his eyes. The last thing he wanted was to say the wrong thing.

Isobel skimmed a hand over Lottie's head, tucking her hair behind her ear. "I certainly hope so."

Lottie nodded, seeming to accept the simple answer. "Can I get a snack before supper?"

"Of course," Isobel said, springing to her feet and fast-walking toward the kitchen.

Cash watched the two of them peer into the pantry, debating the merits of trail mix versus yogurt and blueberries. Lottie's question had served as all the reminder he needed.

The stakes here were life-altering for this child. Nothing else mattered, certainly not his attraction to

Isobel. He would be best served putting a bit of emotional distance between them.

And most definitely keeping his hands to himself.

Men were so much moodier than women.

Sighing, Isobel made her way out to the cabin porch to catch her breath while Lottie took a quick nap before the welcome dinner, and Cocoa ran off some energy out in the yard. Better to be out here with the dog and leave Cash to his mood.

She scooted a rocking chair closer to the rail so she could prop her feet up and appreciate the beautiful view. The music of birds talking back and forth between trees mixed with the light percussion of rustling branches. A stream rippled in the distance. Their little cove felt utterly private, only a hint of voices carrying on the wind.

Had she asked too much of Cash? He'd been the perfect traveling companion for two days straight. Especially for a bachelor. In a minivan. With a kid and a dog.

But shortly after he unloaded the luggage, he'd grown distant, and she wasn't sure what had caused the shift. She could only respect his need for space, especially after all he'd done for them. Maybe he was just maxed out from pseudo family time.

Guilt piled on top of guilt until she sunk lower in the rocking chair. She considered letting him know it was okay if he left early, but that felt ungrateful, like pushing him away from enjoying a ranch vacation.

Thank goodness the only ADA available cabin for the full summer had been the one with three bedrooms.

Cash could have his space. And after he left, she would use the extra room as an office. Not that she wanted to think of him leaving…

Now she was in a mood too.

Thank goodness the perfect distraction came walking through the forest. Her sister Zelda strolled up the path, a small furry dog in her arms. A Maltese maybe? She wore jean shorts and a tie-dyed shirt with cowboy boots, her sleek brown hair swaying all the way down her back. Zelda. As free-spirited as ever. Unchanging, like the vintage Volkswagen convertible she still drove. And seeing her, so familiar, somehow the years apart faded away.

Waving, Zelda sprinted to close the last fifty feet and cheered, "You're really here!"

Isobel leapt to her feet and jogged down the wheelchair ramp to the picket fence. She swung open the gate with a long creak, careful to keep Cocoa behind her. "Come in. Yes, we arrived about forty-five minutes ago."

Zelda angled into the yard, still holding her pup and a brown paper sack. "I can't believe you got here while I was gone. I raced back over as fast as I could—well, stopping on the way to pick up this." She held up the bag. "Dog treats from Bone Appétit for your Cocoa and my Maisey. Are they okay to play together?"

Maisey wriggled free and to the ground. After a quick sniff, Cocoa gave a play bow of acceptance before another word could be said, new best buddies. They sprinted around a fat oak tree, Cocoa adjusting her speed, jogging ahead and racing back to accommodate Maisey's shorter legs.

That settled, Isobel hauled her sister in for a hug, fierce and timeless, before they both eased back and she took the doggie gift. "Thank you for the treats. You've always been so thoughtful."

"It brings me joy," Zelda answered, sitting on the top step by the wheelchair ramp.

Isobel didn't bother telling her there was already a bag in their welcome basket. Zelda wouldn't know since she hadn't been inside her cabin yet. "Did you get the code to your lock?"

"I sure did." She patted her back pocket, her cell phone just peeking out. "Where is that precious niece of mine? I can't wait to spoil her rotten."

"She's taking a nap before the supper party." Isobel sat beside her on the rough planked step, shoulder to shoulder. Was their grandmother smiling down on them? It felt that way.

"I'll have to be patient, I guess. I can hardly believe it's been—what?—two years since I last saw her. Thank goodness for FaceTime."

How would Gran have felt about a FaceTime family connection?

The drumming of dog paws sounded up the wheelchair ramp as Cocoa led the way. The two dogs flopped onto the porch behind them where they sat on the steps.

Isobel reached to greet the little Maltese, pushing to climb past the chocolate Labrador. "And this cutie pie must be the pup you adopted from the shelter?" Upon closer look, the dog was older than she would have guessed since Zelda hadn't owned her for long. Cataracts dulled the brown eyes, and the blond fur was decidedly gray around the muzzle. "How's, uh, Colin? That's his name, right?"

"We broke up a while ago." Zelda bit her lip. Hard.

"I'm sorry." Isobel squeezed her sister's arm, unsure if she should hug her or offer margaritas. "Or is this good news?"

Zelda hesitated, scuffing the toe of her boots through the dirt, her glittery toenail polish dulling like Maisey's eyes. "I'm the one who ended things, and it was the correct decision."

"Even the right choice can be painful." Isobel knew that all too well from her divorce. She also remembered how hard it was to share that pain. As if the loss wasn't bad enough, embarrassment was made worse by well-meaning platitudes.

Zelda scrunched her nose. "I guess we Dalton girls just don't have much luck in the boyfriend department."

Not a subject she wanted to explore further.

"Let's give the dogs some of these—"

Her words were cut short by the slam of the screen door, giving her only a moment's warning before Cash stepped out on the porch. He'd changed for the supper party, looking for all the world like a cowboy, his broad shoulders filling out a plaid shirt. He even held a Stetson in his hands.

Zelda gasped beside her, then let out a low chuckle. "Well, hold your horses. Apparently not all the Dalton sisters are in a dry spell."

Isobel cut her off short, whispering and praying

Cash couldn't overhear. "He's a friend. And he's a boy. But that's it."

Winking mischievously, Zelda slowly rose to her feet. "And here I thought Gran was the only one who told fairy tales."

Chapter Five

An hour later walking to the welcome dinner, Cash still hadn't sorted out how to balance his friendship with his attraction to Isobel. At least she was occupied catching up with her sister, so he had a breather to sift through his feeling, crucial for peace when he said goodbye in a couple of weeks.

The two sisters walked shoulder to shoulder under a bower of trees, chatting nonstop. Zelda pushed the wheelchair along the smooth planked path with Cocoa trotting alongside. Lottie chimed in to talk about her school, her friends and her birthday party, followed by showing off her pink ankle boots with silver studs, matching jeans and a dude ranch T-shirt. So cute she melted his heart.

Like her mom.

He hoped her siblings could be a support for Isobel, in part so he could move on guilt-free. The women definitely resembled each other, even though Zelda had more of a hippie vibe while Isobel was the girl-next-door type. Both beautiful. Objectively speaking. But his gaze kept gravitating back to Isobel. The sway of her hips in slim-cut jeans, a blue flowered shirt tucked

into the waistband with a wide leather belt. Her cowgirl hat rested against her back, held in place by the
string around her neck. Isobel looked mouthwateringly
farm fresh.

Focus forward, he reminded himself, boots thudding
on the wooden walkway. Best to soak up the R and R
of this place before he returned to the job. Isobel didn't
need him anymore.

Straight ahead, the main lodge loomed, a two-story
log structure, with wings off either side. From the ranch's
map legend, he knew one section included guest rooms,
and the other housed the owners and their children.
The center of the lodge sported a dining hall, industrial
kitchen and commons area for gatherings.

And out front, a mini town square was alive with
guests and staff. The scent of grilled meat wafted from
a vintage covered wagon—a chuckwagon, according to
the lettering along the canvas perched off to one side.
Tables with red checkered tablecloths were filled with
a buffet of covered dishes. The massive chalkboard
menu noted s'mores for dessert at the bonfire.

The flames licked up toward the sky, where stars
were just beginning to wink down. The ranch's welcome dinner took place once a week outside the main
lodge, where everyone dressed up in Western gear.
Cowboy garb shouldn't be a big deal for them, coming
from Montana, but here on an actual working ranch,
the cowboy vibe was next level.

The resort's town square was filled with guests and
staff, name tags identifying the employees. Down to

earth, utterly peaceful and blessedly lacking in the flicker and glare of digital technology.

Lottie secured her hat on her head. "Yeehaw, we made it just in time. Didn't we, Aunt Zelda?"

"We sure did," Zelda said.

Isobel held a finger to her pretty lips. "It looks like they're stepping up to the mic now."

Cash hauled his gaze off her mouth and to the dais, where a young couple waved their matching Stetsons at the crowd.

The dark-haired man gripped the microphone first. "Welcome to Moonlight Ridge, Tennessee, home of the Top Dog Dude Ranch and the magical Sulis Cave. I'm Jacob O'Brien, and this lovely lady…" He gestured to the woman at his side, her jeans and red plaid shirt matching his. "This beautiful lady is my wife, Hollie, and also the magnificent chef at our Bone Appétit Café. And those four rascals over there are our children."

He motioned to three boys and a little girl with glasses, all wearing dude ranch T-shirts. "When Hollie and I founded the Top Dog Dude Ranch, we planned for it to be more than a vacation spot. We wanted to create a haven, a place of refuge with tools available to enhance your lives. It is our hope that through our enrichment 'pack-tivities' you carry a piece of the Top Dog experience with you when you return home."

Moving closer to her husband, Hollie swept back her dark ponytail. "If you came here with burdens on your heart, we hope that your time here will do more than refresh you, that you'll also find peace."

Cash was all in on that. His heart still felt leagues

behind his body in the healing department. Point him to the pack-tivities.

Jacob slung an arm around his wife's shoulders as he continued. "And if you're wondering where to start, during breakfast tomorrow, there will be a newcomers' session to acquaint you with the many options available at our ranch. Our staff will be there sharing about their specialties, including our expanded spa features and our newly added whitewater rafting guide."

Hollie clapped her hands together. "If you're an early riser, you may want to stop by our baby goat yoga class by the river. Now, without further ado, time to help yourself to our barbecue buffet and enjoy music from our very own Raise the Woof band."

Near the bonfire, a live band leapt onto a flatbed wagon with guitars, a banjo, a fiddle, even a harmonica and washboard. The drummer took his place on a bale of hay, clicking his drumsticks together to set the beat before a country tune filled the early night air.

Isobel cast a smile at him over her shoulder. "Are you ready to eat? This looks much more appetizing than my PBJs and pickles."

A smile kicked in at the memory as they made their way to the line. "I'm partial to your picnics."

Her cheeks pinkened.

Zelda rolled her eyes with a snort. But whatever she'd planned to say was cut short as ranch owner Hollie O'Brien joined them in the line.

"Hello there." Hollie crouched beside Lottie's wheelchair. "I didn't get a chance to introduce myself to this cutie when you checked in. My daughter Ivy is very excited you'll be here for the summer to play with. I see you like the hat we left for you."

"My name is Lottie and I love it. I'm like a real cowgirl." She adjusted the brim before resting a small hand on her dog's head. "Cocoa likes her bandana too, but she can only wear it when she's not working. 'Cause when she's doing her job, she's gotta wear her vest."

Hollie nodded in approval. "She looks very pretty and official. I won't pet her though. I know she's busy." She reached into her leather bag and pulled out a plastic sheriff's star. "I have these for all the kids. Do you plan to go riding at our kids' camp while you're here?"

"Yeehaw," she squealed, her blue-green eyes lighting. "I mean, yes, ma'am."

"That's great." Standing, Hollie motioned to a man two people behind them in line. "Mr. Troy here is our riding instructor for the summer camp. He's a real-life champion rodeo star. You can tell by the brass belt buckle."

"Whoa. Cool."

The rodeo star ambled closer and tipped his hat to Lottie, then Zelda. "I'll be on the lookout for you, little darlin'."

Lottie shifted in her chair. "Aunt Zelda, are you gonna come watch me ride?"

Zelda flinched, just a hint of wince, before a quick smile covered her discomfort over something or other. If she didn't like horses, she was in for a miserable summer. "Of course I'll be there."

Hollie looked toward Cash. "Your daughter is absolutely precious."

Here they went again. He needed to wear a sign that read: Not the father. Cash pulled a polite smile. "I'm a friend of the family."

"Oh my," she said apologetically, glancing from Isobel to Cash, then back again. "I'm sorry. I just assumed…"

Isobel waved a dismissive hand as they shuffled forward in the line. "Please don't give it another thought. I'm so thankful that you're coordinating a donor drive in your rodeo event this weekend."

"We're happy to help," Hollie said, fidgeting with two more plastic stars. "Your grandmother was a delightful woman. People in Moonlight Ridge speak so fondly of her."

Cash stepped closer, wondering if finding clues about Alice Dalton's past could be this easy. "You knew her?"

"Not personally, but Alice and I chatted a few weeks ago about her provision in her will. She wanted to make sure we were on board to accommodate all three sisters." Hollie shot another look of curiosity at Cash.

Isobel rested a hand on Hollie's arm, angling sideways as two teens ran past, their little brother trailing them toward the crackling bonfire, a smoky scent in the air. "Do you know anything about the child she gave up for adoption?"

Hollie shook her head, ponytail swishing. "I'm as in the dark as you are. But I'm dedicated to helping however I can."

"Thank you." Isobel pressed a hand to her heart. "The accommodations are perfect."

"We're always looking for ways to improve. Like

upgrading the cabin locks," Hollie said, angling to look past Isobel. "Zelda, have you had any more trouble with your door? I'm so sorry it proved tricky."

"All set," Zelda said smartly. "I was just, uh, distracted, after the long trip."

Troy angled closer, winking Zelda's way. "I offered to help, but she's a lady who knows her own mind."

Zelda frowned, crossing her arms. Angry at such an innocuous comment?

Or maybe he was just imagining an undercurrent since his libido had been on overdrive around Isobel lately. Regardless, he was saved from digging deeper for an answer as they reached the front of the chow line.

At least he could feed one hunger this evening.

Troy Shaw was on a dating hiatus for the summer. Not by choice but by necessity.

He'd taken the summer gig at the ranch as a reputation makeover, and Zelda Dalton was already proving to be a major distraction from his goal.

As he downed a second helping of barbecue by the fire, her laugh drew his attention just as much as the sight of her long legs in those cutoff shorts as she set two marshmallows on fire. Squealing, she held up her skewer, blowing on the flame until the gooey mess was safe to eat, gobbling the charred glob with an unmistakable pleasure that sent a bolt of longing through him.

Zelda wasn't his usual type, but she was pretty in a way that said she didn't care what others thought. She dressed to please herself. And that was far more attractive than any runway getup. He hadn't been able to get her out of his mind all afternoon. And that presented a problem.

He finished off an ear of corn, spices and butter exploding on his taste buds, the excellent meal preparation one of the best bonuses about this job at Top Dog. In his past month working here, he'd held firm to his plan of refraining from dating, not in the least tempted by any of the guests, even when a couple of them made their interest abundantly clear.

Sure, he was not a saint by any means. During his younger years on the rodeo circuit, he'd deserved the bad rap. But not so much anymore. Still, the rumors took on a life of their own. Most of the time he didn't care. But once he'd gained full-time custody of his teenage daughter, he'd needed to make a work change. Buying a training camp would allow him to continue using the rodeo skills he loved, while spending less time on the road so he could be there for his kid.

Buying a facility required funding. And the interested financier needed to see he was worth the risk. Thus, the reputation makeover. He just had to hold strong for a week or two around Zelda Dalton until she went back to wherever she came from once her vacation ended.

Tossing his paper plate into the fire, he stood to pluck up a skewer for himself only to find his seat taken and nowhere left except next to Zelda. "Glad everything worked out for you, with the lock and all. A frustrating start to your vacation, no doubt."

She looked up with startled eyes as she unwrapped a mini chocolate bar. "Thank you."

Not much of a talker, was she? He stabbed two marsh-mallows on the spike and held it over the fire, just above the flame. "I realized after the fact that you must have worried about me being privy to your cabin code." He regretted not handling the introduction better. He wasn't a green kid by any means, but when he'd seen her stand-ing there on her porch, his brain cells seemed to have taken a hike for the hills. "I should have identified my-self as an employee."

She quirked her eyebrow, smashing her s'more to-gether. "That would have been helpful. Not that I would have taken you at your word though. Anyone in a cow-boy hat can claim to work here."

"True enough." Smart woman, who also had a deeply wary look darkening her pretty blue-green eyes, mak-ing the reflected flames all the brighter. "You're not much of a trusting soul."

"And you're making assumptions. Such as assuming I'm on vacation. I work at the ranch too." She took a bite of the graham cracker treat with a self-satisfied smirk.

Seriously? Not a guest? But an employee too, and all that entailed for being at the same functions for his entire summer? So much for only needing to hold strong for a week or two. Sure, he thrived on a chal-lenge in the rodeo ring, but the stakes here were too high. His daughter was already acting out to the point of being picked up by the police for truancy last spring. He needed to do whatever it took to give her the sta-bility she needed.

"I stand corrected, ma'am. I guess that means I'll be seeing you around the ranch." He pulled his skewer away from the flame, wishing it could be that simple to distance himself from the smoking hot temptation of this woman.

"The end," Isobel said, closing the Paddington Bear storybook as she sat on the edge of Lottie's bed. She kissed her daughter on the forehead, the scent of baby shampoo sweet and familiar. "Now, go on to sleep. We have a big day ahead of us tomorrow with horseback riding and a visit with your new doctor. I love you."

"Love you too, Mommy," she said, wrapping her arms around Isobel's neck and squeezing hard. "Give Cocoa a kiss night-night, too."

Laughing softly, Isobel pressed her fingers to her mouth, then rubbed the top of the dog's head. "Keep watch over my girl, Cocoa."

The chocolate lab snuggled closer to Lottie's side, like an extra rail. Even though Isobel kept a monitor on so her daughter could call for her, Cocoa also knew to bark for help if necessary. The pup was a godsend.

Standing, Isobel made a quick sweep through the room, picking up clothes and a damp towel. She set the pink Stetson on the stuffed bear in the corner. The bedroom sported rustic decor, log walls and daisy-patterned linens. The bed was rustic pine with built-in rails. She appreciated that the ADA compliant room hadn't simply rolled in a hospital bed. Instead, the furniture matched the other cabins, so Lottie still had the same dude ranch vacation experience rather than staying in a space that resembled a medical facility.

Laundry basket under her arm, she clicked off the

wagon wheel lamp. The night-light cast circling stars on the ceiling while emitting the white noise of a babbling brook.

"Mommy," Lottie said, stopping her at the door, "who are my doctors gonna be here?"

The worry in the child's voice added concern to her own. She thought they'd gone over it enough to allay her daughter's fears, but apparently not. She sagged back against the wall, hugging the laundry basket.

"Honey, remember, it's all in your tablet, their names and their pictures. We're going to meet Dr. Barnett tomorrow." Dr. Barnett had come highly recommended, a pediatrician with a thriving practice in Chattanooga before relocating to Moonlight Ridge. He was a general practitioner now. She'd heard he made the change to have more time since he'd become the primary caretaker for his two grandchildren. "And guess what? Dr. Barnett lives right next to the ranch. His wife is the stable manager. They have kids you can play with too, like Hollie's children."

"That's nice." She pleated the sheet between her fingers, her forehead furrowed with a determination that hinted she wasn't satisfied with the answer yet. "Are they *all* good doctors? As good as the ones I had back home, who know when to give me stickers so I don't cry?"

Having a child with a chronic health problem broke her heart in a million ways. There was much she couldn't change, so she doubled down on details she could control.

"Oh, sweetie, I promise I checked them all out." Isobel placed the basket back on the floor and returned to sit on the edge of the mattress again. "Your doctors at home handpicked each new physician for you. They even called them personally to let them know we're here for the summer and how much they adore you."

"No waiting list? Pinky swear?" Lottie asked, her hair still damp and in braids for the night. "'Cause what if I got sick before I get to meet 'em all?"

"Pinky swear. No waiting list." And that, in and of itself, was a major miracle. Their primary care physician back in Minnesota had gone to Vanderbilt for medical school and still had connections in the area. "We would not have come here until that was settled."

"But what if I need that kidney? And I can't remember my new doctors' names?" Such big worries for such a young child.

Isobel's heart broke a little more. But the last thing she wanted was for her child to see her fears. "That's why I'll be right there beside you."

"Will Daddy come?" Her voice wobbled, hopeful and hesitant all at once.

Isobel measured her words. "If he can."

Lottie sighed. "That means no."

Probably. "He has to work, and he works to help take care of you."

"'Cause I need his 'surance.'" Lottie recited the answer Isobel had given countless times. "I know, I know."

"We'll FaceTime him every day." Like they Face-Timed Zelda and Neve? The solution felt more hollow than normal tonight. "We can talk about it more in the morning. Okay?"

Lottie hesitated so long, it seemed she might debate further. Finally, she nodded. "See you in the morning."

"In the morning. Sleep well." Isobel smoothed back Lottie's bangs and pressed another kiss to her forehead.

Isobel sat on the edge of the bed, stroking her daughter's hair until her eyes fluttered closed. Her breaths evened out, the noise machine's water shushing the only other sound in the room. Incrementally, Isobel stood, tiptoed across the floor and picked up the laundry basket. As she eased into the hallway, she cast one last look at her child.

Lottie turned her head to bury her face in Cocoa's side, her voice a muffled whisper, just barely distinguishable. "It's not fair."

Forget about her heart breaking. The whole organ shattered. Was Lottie thinking about all the normal childhood things she couldn't do? The sports and games she missed out on with differently abled peers? Or was she thinking about how little she saw her dad or how much time she had to devote to thinking about her health and just moving through her days?

Because her daughter was right. None of it was fair. Isobel thought she'd come to peace with the fact there were things she couldn't change for her child.

But it still stung her deeply that she couldn't change things. That she couldn't do more to help Lottie through the challenges she faced.

In this moment with the hurt and worry slicing through her, she wanted nothing more than to run to Cash and take the friendship, the support he offered.

Chapter Six

Propping his boots on the porch rail, Cash tipped back a longneck and took in the fireflies sparking up the night like Christmas tree lights come early. He should go to bed. Certainly the day had been long enough. Except experience told him that nightmares powered harder when emotions were high. The combination of returning to work shortly, along with eventually having to say goodbye to Isobel and Lottie, had too many of his feelings simmering just below the surface.

The cabin door creaked behind him. He dropped his feet to the ground, looking over his shoulder to find Isobel slumped against the frame. Her hair flowed loose around her in a mahogany tumble. She'd changed since the dinner, wearing sleep shorts with a sweatshirt, a nod to the chilly mountain evenings.

She looked utterly and completely breathtaking, all the more tempting for the effortlessness.

"Mind if I join you?" she asked, a glass of wine in one hand and a cutting board of cheeses in the other.

"These rocking chairs are the best seats in the house." He gestured to the rough-hewn rocker beside him, standing and taking the cheese board from her.

She started to sit, then paused halfway, standing again. Wine still in hand, she wrapped her arms around him for a fast and fierce hug. One he couldn't return with the tray in one hand and his beer in the other. And just that fast, the embrace was over. She quickly took her seat and sipped her red wine, avoiding his eyes.

Even so, the soft imprint and sweet scent of her lingered in his senses. He set the tray on the end table before reclaiming his seat. It was for the best, since his legs weren't too steady.

Dragging in a ragged breath of air, he rolled his bottle between both palms. "What was that for?"

She met his gaze sheepishly. "Just a thank-you at the end of a long day. I don't know how I would have managed the trip here without your help."

"You'd have made the drive," he said with certainty, reaching for a square of cheddar and a cracker. "It would have been a white-knuckled trip, but you would have done it."

"I'm not just talking about the drive. But being here for moral support." She chewed her bottom lip, darting a look toward the cabin where her child slept. "This kind of relocation is stressful with a kid. But you made it fun for us with your silly songs and bad jokes."

"My silly songs?" He clapped a hand over his chest. "Lady, I'm crushed."

"I'm being serious." She nudged him gently, bumping his elbow off the armrest. "I appreciate the way you delight in Lottie. It's genuine. I see that."

"You've done a good job bringing her up. That kid is going to take the world by storm." He dusted the crumbs off his fingers. "Are you ready now to tell me what really had you so emotional?"

She took her time spreading brie and jam over a baguette slice, as if deciding whether or not to share her thoughts with him. "The enormity of it all hit—of the kidney transplant, new doctors, fear that we won't find an organ donor, then terror that if we do, something could go wrong."

At the mention of the kidney transplant, his throat closed with apprehension. He set aside his beer. "Those are very real concerns."

Her head tipped back against the rocker as she blinked fast, the sheen of tears glinting in the porch light. "Lottie has them too, which makes it all the worse. She knows it's not fair. And that's the part I can't do anything about no matter how hard I try."

Without a second thought, he clasped her hand in his. Holding firm. Silently, while night bugs and bullfrogs continued their chorus. Complimenting her motherhood, telling her she had the best of care wouldn't take away an ounce of worry.

Sometimes distraction was the best course of action. "I spent some time on the internet while you were reading Lottie her bedtime story."

"Oh really?" She looked his way, hands still clasped. "Did you find out something about Gran?"

"No, something else." He squeezed her fingers, surprised at how easy it was to continue the contact. "I pulled up the list of events for the two weeks I'm at the ranch."

"That's great," she said, smiling. "What events did

you choose? I hope it's something totally outrageous and fun. You should make the most of your time here. Please don't feel like you need to look out for us."

"This isn't about me." He shifted in the chair to half face her, his thumb stroking along her wrist. Her pulse leapt under his touch, sparking an answer in his own heart rate. "I want you to select something that's just about you. You deserve to make the most of your time here too."

"You really are a good man." Her eyebrows pinched together as she searched his face. Her eyes held his with an awareness. Their hands linked. The connection added a crackle to the air, the promise of a kiss that hadn't happened but could. All they had to do was lean a few inches closer.

Except holding hands was one thing. Simple. But a kiss? That would complicate matters between them, making the coming weeks and the impending farewell all the tougher. "That doesn't answer my question."

The air sparked for an instant more, as if those lightning bugs populated the air between them. Her exhale puffed lightly into the air like a phantom kiss against his skin.

She squeezed his hand once more before letting go and standing to retrieve her wineglass. "I'll think on it. I'm going to turn in. See you in the morning."

They'd spent a night in two rooms at the hotel, but somehow this was different. Their first time sleeping in the same house, greeting a new day together while sharing coffee. How easy it would be to get used that. Too easy. He needed to focus his energies on helping her enjoy the R and R of this place before he left. He couldn't control the future and the outcome of Lottie's health needs. However, he could do his level best to help Isobel decompress, to recharge before she faced the battle ahead.

Cocoa the Caring Canine

Hugs have a magical power. I learned that in my training to become a service dog.

The hugs I give.

The hugs my person gives me because she needs contact.

The feeling of not being alone.

Because loneliness can hurt every bit as much as an injury, and the comfort of contact with another living being can make the worst pain more tolerable.

That's why we need to treasure our friends. Lottie's mom has the very best pal in the world. He's kept us company for a long time. Six months of people time…

Isobel's hands hovered over the keyboard as she searched for the right words to explain how much that hug, the simple hand-holding on the porch had meant to her. But knowing that Cash would read her words seriously hamstrung her ability to pour her heart into the admission. He would no doubt see through the veil of Cocoa's "voice."

Isobel would have attributed her struggle to the early

hour, but she was used to writing at the crack of dawn. Now, sitting cross-legged in the tangle of red gingham covers on her brass bed, she needed to accept that the words weren't flowing this morning.

The rising sun was just starting to peek between the slats of the wooden shutters covering her window. She didn't have much longer before Lottie woke. Already she could hear Cash stirring in his room next door.

Her phone vibrated on the end table, offering the perfect excuse to abandon her laptop. She angled over to snag it from beside her empty wine glass. A reminder of that unforgettable hug last night.

She knew it was a hug of friendship and something she needed. But the connection rattled her a little too, reminding her how long it had been since…well, since a lot of things. None of which bore thinking about now.

The cell screen scrolled the caller ID. Her ex-husband. Not the distraction she was looking for.

"Hello, Colin," she answered, all business, the best way to handle matters with her ex. No need to state it was too early for a conversation. He frequently lost track of time zones when driving a long haul through the night. "I sent you an email with our itinerary before we left Montana."

"Yes, I saw it," he said, sounds of passing cars and a semi's air horn echoing. "That's not why I'm calling."

It was too early for him to speak with Lottie. "Then, is there something wrong?"

"Can't I phone because I'm missing my best girls? I'm sure Lottie is having a blast. But are you okay?"

She bristled despite the veil of kindness he'd flung over the inquiry.

Why all the sudden interest in her life? Sure, they tried their best to be polite to each other in front of Lottie, but this ventured into unknown territory for them. "I'm thankful that Lottie has the opportunity for such an extravagant summer getaway, with activities geared to accommodate her."

"I wish I could provide more for my family. I'm—"

"Colin, that wasn't what I meant." She didn't want to go down the path of reassuring him. They'd had this conversation so many times, usually leading to him wanting sympathy from her over his long hours. "I know you work hard. We both do. And I know you miss Lottie. I'll try to do better about having her FaceTime you more often."

"That would be great, thanks." He paused to clear his throat three times. A quirk of his right before he launched into a tricky subject. The trait had once been endearing. Not so much anymore. "So, Isobel, I saw the photos on your Cocoa page. When does Cash Warner leave? I thought he was only driving you two out there."

Now they were getting down to the real reason for his call. A reason all the touchier with the sound of Cash moving about the cabin. She drummed her fingers impatiently along the cover of her laptop.

For some reason, Colin seemed to hold out hope they would get back together, even though they'd been divorced for a year. He'd cheated. More than once. And couldn't seem to get it through his head there was no returning to what they'd once shared.

Only because Cash's presence had bearing on Lottie's life did Isobel answer the question. "Since he doesn't start his new job right away, it only made sense for him to enjoy some time at the ranch. It's the least I could offer after he drove me, our child, and our dog halfway across country."

"I should have been there to help you," Colin said in a voice that begged for her to give him reassurances.

Isobel picked at a mermaid sticker a younger Lottie had decorated her laptop with long ago.

"That's not what I said and not what I meant." She thought of how Cash helped without asking for anything in return. And at the end of the day, he still showed concern over her stress level.

"What did you mean, then?" he pressed.

She took three bracing breaths, collecting her temper before answering. Maintaining a civil co-parenting relationship was crucial for Lottie's well-being. "That you don't have the right to question me about who I spend time with."

His low growl on the other end of the line signaled the end of his good-natured wheedling. "When that person's presence affects my daughter—"

"You should probably stop right there." Especially since one of his affairs had been with their daughter's physical therapist. From now on, Isobel would stand her ground with Colin. And not just for herself but for her daughter. To model strength with grace. "I don't think you want to enter a discussion on that subject. You're far from being in a position to judge."

"Fair enough. I'm sorry for upsetting you. Again."

His exhale sounded like a deflating balloon. "Izzy, when are you going to forgive me?"

She'd always hated when he called her that. Why couldn't he remember? It was such a simple thing to ask. "I forgave you a long time ago." And she had. Not just for him, but because forgiving him was crucial to healing the hurt inside herself. But forgiving wasn't the same as forgetting. "That doesn't mean we can go back to the way things were before."

"Of course, of course," he rushed to add so quickly the assurance rang hollow. "Listen, I need to focus on the road. The weather's starting to act up, rain storms and all. Give Lottie a kiss from Daddy and tell her I'll talk to her soon."

The line disconnected before she could respond, because clearly, he'd already decided what he believed. There was no need for her to press. Just continue to hold firm—and hope he stopped calling her Izzy. Which made her think of a school-days bully who'd called her Izzy the Lizard.

She tossed aside her cell phone and reached for her laptop. Quiet time to write was running out, and she needed to make more progress on the blog before Lottie woke. Deleting what she'd typed so far, she gave the subject a fresh spin.

Hugs—from the right individual—have a magical power...

Cash was a "two cups of coffee" kind of guy.
This morning, though, called for at least three mugs.

He drained the last of the java as the muffled pad of footsteps sounded in the hall. Isobel. He'd heard her soft voice a few minutes ago, speaking with someone on the phone. The voice was low and deep. He suspected the caller was her ex-husband, not that it was any of Cash's business.

He just wanted to speak with her before he headed out. Sure, he could leave a note, but yeah, he wanted to see her before he left for the morning.

She joined him beside the coffee maker, still wearing the sleep shorts and loose sweatshirt that made him ache to tunnel up under the waistband and explore her curves. There was something more intimate about a shared morning than a late night drink.

Pivoting away from her, he rinsed his mug in the sink before setting it on the drying rack. "What do you have on tap for this morning?"

She busied herself with pouring her dark roast, adding creamer and two heaping sugars. "We're having breakfast with Zelda before she goes to work. After that I'm taking Lottie to a candle- and soap-making workshop at the greenhouse. The landscaper on staff here was featured in *Better Homes and Gardens*."

Barely pausing to catch her breath, she continued, clinking her spoon against the side as she stirred, "This afternoon, we have an appointment with her new GP, before Neve gets in this evening. Oh, and I need to stop by the library…"

Her list continued in minute detail, the rambling uncharacteristic as she cradled her mug. Was she feeling self-conscious over the hug? From holding hands? To be fair, he wasn't feeling all that steady himself.

"Good luck with all of that." He started to offer to help but thought of how nervous she was of taking advantage, even though he'd never felt that in the least. He reminded himself of his hopes of encouraging her to give herself a break over the next couple of weeks. "I'm taking an early trail ride. Maybe next time you can join me."

He didn't give her a chance to answer—or turn him down. He gave her shoulder a passing squeeze on his way to the door. As he'd done dozens of times. But somehow the casual touch charged the air in a way it never had before.

Outside, he grabbed his knees and willed away the stars behind his eyelids. Three deep breaths later, he sprinted down the porch ramp and opened the fence gate.

Sidestepping morning walkers with their dogs, he jogged down the well-marked path, following the paw signs leading to the stables, three barns and a mini arena. Even what appeared to be a little petting zoo, complete with goats and pigs. He'd found the lodge and little town square impressive. The riding opportunities were next-level incredible, the trails nestled in the mountainside and foothills in a natural tableau that kept the place from looking resort-like. The whole ranch gave the appearance of a more homestyle operation.

A very large home spread.

The green pasture was alive and ready for the day, horses nibbling on grass. Guests already lined up at the stable door. Staff, identifiable by their identical blue shirts, moved in and out of the barn in a synchronized rhythm of tending the animals and the guests in equal measure.

Looking out at the sunrise cresting over the main stable, he was overwhelmed by a deep gratitude that he'd survived that fire to see this morning. And an even deeper guilt that his friend Elijah had not. When would that ease? He didn't have a clue.

"Hey there, can I help you find something?" Troy Shaw ambled closer, leading a pony with an adaptive saddle.

Lottie would love this. Cash hoped he had the opportunity to see her ride before he left. "All's good. I'm just taking in the view before the morning trail ride. Working on living in the moment rather than tapping my foot waiting in line."

"The ranch is packed full of those incredible views." Troy draped the pony's lead over the fence post. "Speaking of savoring the moment, did you check out the breakfast buffet?"

Cash stroked the pony's silky muzzle. "Our pantry is well stocked." He'd finished off two granola bars while trying not to think about overhearing Isobel's early phone call as he headed to the kitchen and wondering if she'd spoke with her ex-husband. "I wanted to get an early start to make the trail ride."

"You've got about fifteen minutes until check in." Troy motioned toward the stable where Jacob O'Brien mounted a quarter horse with ease. "The boss usually takes a quick scope of the land on his own before leading a group."

"I need all the exercise I can get with the great food served around here," Cash said with a laugh, only half joking. He needed to stay in top shape for his return to work, for safety's sake.

"It's one of the many great perks of being employed at the ranch. Free room and board." Troy nodded toward the teenage girl about ten yards away sitting on the split rail fence listening to earbuds. "That young lady—avoiding work—is my daughter. She's actually my reason for leading the kids' camp this summer."

"How so?" Cash hitched his foot on the bottom rung, sticking to his vow to live in the moment. No rushing around. Living the Top Dog Dude Ranch code, so to speak.

"The rodeo circuit is no place to bring up a kid." Troy scrubbed a hand over his jaw. "I've tried taking Harper on the road with me and homeschooling her. The travel was supposed to be an education too."

"I'm assuming it didn't work out as planned?" His thoughts flew to Isobel and all the sacrifices she made to be there for her child.

"Not by a long shot," he said, with a dry chuckle. "She wants those regular high school experiences— friends, going to a dance, stuff like that. And the last thing I want is for her to find a 'friendship' with some young rodeo hotshot."

Sounded like the guy was speaking from experience. Cash had always kept his love life simple. One woman at a time. "You're in a tough spot. What happens after the summer camp is over?"

"I'm planning to start a training complex of my own.

That will give Harper the stability she needs and I get to keep on doing what I love. It's a win-win."

"Sounds like you've got it all planned out." Maybe Cash misjudged the guy. Maybe he wasn't a player after all, but more like a real family man. The sort that Isobel needed and deserved to have in her life.

And that very thought made Cash want to keep Isobel far away from the stables.

"I'm trying to get my ducks in a row. But sometimes life throws a curveball," Troy said wryly, folding his arms along the top of the split rail fence "So what's the deal with Isobel Dalton's sister Zelda?"

Chapter Seven

"Zelda, thanks for tagging along for the kiddie craft hour," Isobel said as she slid on a bench with her sister in a far corner of the greenhouse. "I'm sure it's not how you envisioned spending your lunch break."

"I'm exactly where I want to be," Zelda said, opening her boxed lunch, a cardboard container covered in a pattern of pawprints and horseshoes. Her hair was smoothed back in a French braid for work. "As much as I love my job, it smells a lot better in here than in the grooming salon."

Grow lights hummed overhead, casting a warm glow over rows of flowers and greenery, from lilacs to ferns. From hanging baskets along the rafters to pots in stands. Bundles of drying herbs and blooms hung upside down from hooks. A gurgling fountain was made of a rustic pump flowing into a large bucket.

The place smelled like heaven. "I have to confess, I could sit here all day doing absolutely nothing, knowing my child is happily occupied."

Off to one side, three long tables were filled with children choosing and mixing their own recipe of scents.

Lottie scooped a heaping spoonful of rose petals and poured them into her basket.

More children packed the bench seats. Some of the kids were guests. Others she recognized from last night's dinner event. The O'Briens' four children. And triplet boys, the gift shop manager's sons. And all seven gathered around and across from Lottie. And a little vacationer, Sebastian, who was forever being ditched by his teenage sisters at any event that included childcare. He was a sweet kid though, and Lottie enjoyed him.

Her daughter was fast on her way to making new friends, judging by the way they passed baskets around, laughing together over spilled potpourri.

Relaxing into her chair, Isobel shifted to face her sister. "How was your morning on the new job? You sure jumped right in quickly."

Zelda dusted breadcrumbs off her Top Dog employee shirt. "The need was there—as in they needed the extra hands and I needed the extra money."

"If there's any way that I can help…"

"I'm fine, really. Money was just tight after my breakup. The apartment was in his name, and I had to relocate. All those hookup fees were tough when I wasn't getting anything back from the deposits on the place I'd just left."

"That feels unfair." Guilt pinched Isobel that she hadn't known about any of this at the time Zelda was dealing with it.

"I needed a clean break. It was worth all the overtime at the grooming salon back home to be free of him."

The phrasing of her sister's words caught her off

guard. Clearly there had been a darker side to the relationship. "I didn't realize it was that bad—"

"Let's not talk about me," Zelda cut her off. She passed a cluster of green grapes from her box lunch over to Isobel. "I'd much rather hear about you and that sexy firefighter."

Isobel popped a grape from the stem and wondered if she should press her sister more about her life. But maybe Zelda was grateful for the time away from the problems back home.

"I could continue to repeat myself—he's just a friend. But it's clear you're not going to believe me." Lifting her thermos of coffee, she eyed her sister over the rim of the cup. "So, instead, let's talk about all those undercurrents with you and the rodeo guy?"

"You mean the big obnoxious cowboy? I'm done with men who think they know it all." Zelda crunched a chip with vengeance.

"Your breakup was that bad? I'm so sorry." She covered her sister's hand, reminded of the year Zelda got stood up for prom. Isobel had planned to go stag with friends, so they'd folded Zelda into their group. Zelda had still ended up in the bathroom crying.

Silence settled between them, broken only by the gurgle of the fountain and the giggles of children concocting their bottles of homemade bubble bath. Cocoa rested under the table, her nose twitching overtime at all the smells.

Seeing the kids take joy in such a down-to-earth craft reminded her of summers at Gran's farm, magical and wonderfully messy. Maybe that would be a safer topic than men. "Remember when Gran gave us each a baby chick to raise to teach us responsibility?"

Zelda snorted on a laugh as she chewed her sub, then pressed a napkin to her mouth as she swallowed. "To keep us busy, more likely."

"That too," Isobel conceded. "And there was the night we decided to take her entire stash of candy since, usually, she doled it out to us one piece at time."

"It was at the top of the pantry and Neve tripped, making all sorts of noise."

"You were a stellar actress—" Isobel pointed at her sister "—stumbling around and pretending to be groggy while we ran and hid the bag."

"Only to find out later we'd actually taken a sack of pecans that hadn't even been shelled yet." Zelda rolled her eyes.

"I've always thought Gran knew what we were up to, but she never let on." If only they'd known how much more Gran kept hidden behind her lighthearted facade. "It's still surreal to learn she had this whole other life. Do you think Gran's story about the lost puppy was about her son?"

Zelda's eyebrows lifted in surprise before she shrugged. "Could have been."

"Why didn't she just tell us?" Isobel wondered if she'd let her grandmother down somehow, being so wrapped up in her own life that she wasn't in tune to Gran, like that child in search of candy, stumbling around in the dark.

"I guess we'll never know." Zelda's fatalistic words hung between them.

"We may never know the reason, but I refuse to give up without finding her child and every single one of his descendants." If she had to tear apart the library, the whole town even, she would leave no stone left unturned.

The early morning ride had cleared Cash's head, leaving him even more determined to help Isobel enjoy something recreational at the ranch, all on her own. But apparently, convincing her would be tougher than he'd expected.

At least she'd let him tag along and keep her company while Lottie enjoyed story time at the ranch's small library because her new friends were attending— including another camper named Sebastian. They seemed to have a crush on each other.

Pushing the chair up the ramp, Cash listened to Isobel's strategy for searching records. The library resembled an old clapboard schoolhouse, with a bell mounted to the roof. Quaint, like the rest of this town, like a fairy tale. And Isobel looked the part of a cowgirl princess in her long lacy dress with brown leather boots. They walked side by side, the brush of her skirt like a phantom touch.

As he guided the wheelchair up the library's ramp, Cash angled down to speak to Lottie. "How did your morning go with your mom and your aunt?"

Lottie glanced back, her ponytail swishing. "They drank coffee the whole time and talked. But me and my new friends made candles and bath salts that smell really good." She reached into the pouch on the arm of her chair and pulled out a small bottle filled with clear liquid and floating petals. "Here. This bubble bath is for you to thank you for driving us here. It's s'posed to help with sore muscles. I thought maybe it would help 'cause you got hurt in that big fire."

"Thank you." Touched by the child's thoughtfulness, he admired the bottle carefully labeled in Lottie's handwriting. "This is the best gift anyone has ever given me."

"And you'll smell like flowers too."

Isobel's soft laugh teased him. "Can't wait to check that out."

He angled to whisper in her ear. "Hey, don't make fun of my gift. Now, go get started on your search, and I'll make sure Lottie has the best seat in the house for story time."

Giving Isobel a quick wink, he strode through the electric doors, Cocoa keeping pace. The cool blast of the air conditioner hit his face, along with the scent of books. So many books.

Isobel pointed toward the far corner where children gathered in a cluster on an ABC mat. "That must be where we're supposed to go. There are the O'Brien kids and the gift shop manager's triplets."

"Why don't you go ahead and start at a computer station? I'll get her settled," Cash said, moving past before she could argue. Navigating around a cart and shelves, he was reminded of trips to the library with his father. They'd searched for every children's book available on firefighters. Full of the memory, he was thankful to be able to give Lottie a similar experience today.

He lifted her from the chair to settle her on the mat.

She was so light, he wanted to hug her close and shield her from the world. He would have given anything to be a donor match for her.

"Thanks, Cash. You're the best."

Cocoa settled beside her, pressed up close to her outstretched legs. Cash scratched the dog on the head. "Look after our girl, okay?"

The dog blinked her wide brown eyes in acknowledgment, the deep love for Lottie shining through.

Satisfied the child was secure, he found Isobel at a computer screen, her fingers flying across the keyboard.

"How's it going?" he asked, pulling up a rolling chair beside her, their shoulders close enough to feel her warmth.

"Laborious." She typed faster, shoulder bumping him. "I'm looking through old high school yearbooks during Gran's time to see if they have any prom photos. At the very least, I hope to compile a list of names for people I can speak with about her."

Cash exhaled a gust, not that it helped sweep away the attraction. But moving would only draw attention to their proximity. "What can I do to help?"

"As I make the list, could you run a search to see who's still living and if they're in the area?" She nodded toward the computer station next to her.

"I'm on it." He rolled his chair over, wondering if she'd been affected too.

Then the lights dimmed to half power for the start of story time, and a screen to the side lit up with an image of a cave, with a lush mountain backdrop. He never would have expected to find a library romantic. But then he'd never been to the library with Isobel before.

For a moment, he allowed himself to be distracted by the story time visible just over the top of the screen.

The librarian wore a fairy princess costume with a fur trimmed cape and a tiara. She held her scruffy, small dog under her arm. The pooch sported a ruffled jester collar with bells.

"My name is Susanna and this little fellow is Atlas. He comes to all my story times. I'm the librarian at the elementary school, but I do story time here as well, especially in the summer. How many of you are here on vacation?"

Approximately half of the children raised their hands, waggling their fingers in the air, including Lottie's little friend Sebastian. His teenage sisters had dropped him off at the story time before running off clutching their backpacks, swimming goggles dangling from the straps.

His mind went back to all the times his father had taken him to the library to choose firefighter books, but for some reason Cash couldn't recall if there had been story time during those outings. Yet another thing he would never be able to ask his father or his mother. They'd died in a simple car wreck when a driver in the oncoming lane fell asleep at the wheel, drifting into their lane.

Wiping out all of Cash's family in seconds.

He hauled his focus back to the present, determined to make the most of his time with Isobel and Lottie.

"Well, today," the librarian said, settling into a rocking chair, her dog in her lap, "I'm going to share a favorite story of local kids. It's a legend of Moonlight Ridge's very own Sulis Springs Cave. It goes all the way back to the many great-grandpas of Mr. Jacob O'Brien, who owns the dude ranch."

The children squealed and applauded, their little hands releasing the scent of flower petals and scented oils that survived multiple washings.

Isobel paused her typing, angling back to watch for a moment alongside him. A beautiful smile spread across her face as she got swept up in the tale, the storyteller in her clearly engaged.

Brains and beauty. A dangerous combination.

Maybe he should pay attention to the legend as well.

Susanna leaned forward even though the children were laser-focused on her. "Once upon a time, when my ancestors were settling into this area from Scotland and Ireland, they followed a doe to the cave opening. It wasn't just any old doe though. She was the Queen of the Forest, who glowed like starlight…"

The screen behind her flickered with changing images to follow her tale. "The O'Brien ancestors knew the type of animal well. They used to roam Scotland and lead wayward souls to safe places and healing water. They offered respite. A way to connect. You see, my ancestors were struggling to get settled in this region. Many challenges almost broke them. They wanted to give up on the land. On each other. But they followed the Queen of the Forest to the cave mouth."

She cradled her dog Atlas closer. "There was a lost pup in the cave that needed attention. So, while they waited for a pot of coffee to brew over the fire, they cleaned up the young pup. As they rinsed the puppy, their bond was renewed. Healed. They found a way to work with the land, with each other."

A collage of images sped through, from grainy black-and-white images to sepia tones, through the years, showing the growth of Moonlight Ridge all the way to the present-day dude ranch, with animals grazing and the lush floral landscape.

Isobel sat up straighter beside him. "Did you see that?"

"Yeah," he said, spinning his chair to face her. "Nice montage."

"No," she said, shaking her head vehemently, her eyes wide. "I meant did you see the photo in the middle of the slide show...the old image with a young couple in a canoe. I could swear that's my grandmother."

An hour later on her way to Lottie's doctor checkup, Isobel still couldn't calm the nervous hope in her gut. She gripped the wheel, thankful the drive to Dr. Barnett's office followed a mostly wide road without sharp turns.

Sure, an old photo wasn't much to go on, but she'd spoken with the librarian afterward, who provided her source for the image. The more Isobel looked at the picture, the more she became convinced a younger Gran was staring back at her. If so, it was her first tangible connection to her grandmother living here, beyond a simple name and address in the census. Cash had generously offered to keep digging since she had to leave for Lottie's new-patient appointment with Dr. Barnett.

"Mommy," Lottie chimed from the back seat. "Would the special waters at Sulis Springs make me all better?"

Isobel hadn't considered her daughter would glean that from story time. How she wished she could offer Lottie a magical cure. "The sulfur springs make people feel better. It's like when you soak in a warm bath after a long PT session."

"Then why do they call them healing waters?" Lottie's face scrunched up in the rearview mirror.

"That's a good question," Isobel answered as she turned into the parking lot outside the doctor's office—located in a small renovated train station. "There are all sorts of ways to think about the word 'healing.' It can also mean when your heart is happier. The legend of this place talks about how its special magic helps people put aside their 'worries.'"

"Mama, maybe you need to get in the springs too then, because you worry about me a lot," Lottie said, her voice soft.

Putting the van in Park and turning off the ignition, Isobel pivoted to face her daughter. "*All* mamas worry. It comes with the job description of being a parent."

Lottie shook her head, ponytail swishing faster than the dog's tail. "Daddy doesn't worry, and he's a parent."

"Of course he does." She knew Colin cared about Lottie. He worked hard to be a good provider and stay in touch.

"Not like you do," Lottie said, unwavering. "Can we go to the water sometime? Please?"

"Of course." An easy enough request. "I would love to."

"Can Cash come too?" Lottie skimmed her fingers

along the top of Cocoa's head. "I bet it would make his leg and his arm and his heart feel better."

A lump formed in Isobel's throat. She appreciated Lottie's warm nature and kind spirit, but was it a mistake to allow her to grow so close to Cash? Would the loss of their friend leave a hole in her heart?

"I'll ask, but he may already have plans. He's trying to make the most of the ranch activities before he leaves."

"Wait, what? He's going? When?"

She'd told her about that, hadn't she? Isobel wondered if she'd been so focused on ignoring the attraction to Cash that she'd lost sight of communicating his leaving to her daughter.

"Soon, sweetie. He was never going to stay. He just drove us out here so I didn't have to tow the trailer by myself along those mountain roads." She didn't want to think about when the time came to return home. In fact, she didn't want to think about Cash leaving at all. "We need to get inside before we're late for your doctor's appointment."

The most important part of her day. Everything else needed to move to the back burner.

In short order, she unloaded Lottie and Cocoa, then made fast tracks along the paved sidewalk. The old rails were visible next to the brick walkway, the simple kind from around 1900, according to the brass plaque. Old tracks ran behind the former train station, but everything else had been modernized on the street…and inside.

Like the rest of Moonlight Ridge, the waiting room

was utterly charming. Vintage park benches had been restored and lined the walls. A toy train track ran along the top of the wall, the choo-choo chugging along in a circle, music playing softly. The area was spotless yet somehow didn't carry the antiseptic scent of many medical facilities.

While her daughter chattered excitedly nonstop to Cocoa, Isobel barely had time to sign in and sit before the grandmotherly receptionist called Lottie's name. They were guided to an exam room that was clearly meant to appeal to the younger patients. The exam table had a steam engine attached to the front, and a mural covered one wall of a mountain with train tracks weaving through. And were there hints of the legend of Sulis Springs, the cave guarded by a green dragon with a stag and puppy on the ridge line?

Pretty. But a touch of vertigo shook the ground under Isobel's feet.

The door opened again to admit a distinguished gentleman in green surgical scrubs, dark-haired with silver at the temples. From her internet research about the new physicians, Isobel recognized him right away.

"Hello, Miss Lottie." He thrust out a hand to her daughter first, then Isobel. "I'm Dr. Barnett. It's a pleasure to meet you both."

Isobel smiled her gratitude. "Thank you for seeing us on such short notice."

"I had a spot open up with one of my patients moving out of town."

Another perfect timing coincidence.

Lottie reached into her sack on the arm of her chair

and pulled out her tablet to show Dr. Barnett. "My mommy put pictures of my new doctors on here beside photos of my old doctors and therapists back at home. That way I'll know what you're s'posed to do for me."

Dr. Barnett nodded approvingly, his demeanor easygoing but his eyes keen, assessing the new patient. "That's very helpful. I'm going to share that great idea with some other patients of mine. Your mom sounds like a super parent."

Isobel squirmed under the praise. She tried her best but, at the end of the day, felt she'd fallen short. Maybe once a kidney donor had been found and the surgery was complete, she could rest easier. "Lottie and I are a good team."

Dr. Barnett reached into a drawer under the sink and pulled out a roll of cartoon stickers. "What do you say we let your mother pick a sticker too?"

Lottie beamed, pointing to two unicorns. "Yay, we can match."

Dr. Barnett peeled two off the roll. "The unicorn is my little Mavis's favorite, too."

Lottie pressed her sticker on her shirt and passed the other to her mom. "Doctor, you've got kids? I wish I had a baby brother or a baby sister. My mom says I'm all the family she needs."

That stung more than alcohol on a cut. Her mind swirled with long-ago dreams of four children gathered around the Christmas tree. She hadn't allowed herself to think of that image in years.

Isobel rested a hand on her daughter's arm, grateful for the family she had. "That's enough, sweetie. Dr.

Barnett needs to get to work so he can see the rest of the people with appointments."

"I'm here to listen anytime. It's one of the things I like most about being a small-town doctor," he said, sliding his stethoscope along Lottie's back. "Breathe in… Breathe out. Again… I get to know my patients. Lottie—and you—are now my patients."

Lottie high-fived him. "That's right."

Dr. Barnett draped his stethoscope around his neck again and level a pointed look at Isobel. "And don't forget to look after your own health. It's easy to become so busy caring for others that you forget about yourself."

She understood what he said, but the implementation…not so easy. Something else to put on her to-do list for once the kidney transplant was behind them. "I hear you."

"Good," he said, setting the chart on the counter. "If you have any questions or concerns, call my office or reach out to my wife at the ranch. And please do let me know how you like your new PT assignment."

How strange that until now she hadn't thought of going to PT here—without Cash being there waiting.

Isobel settled into a seat in the corner while Dr. Barnett completed the exam, coaxing smiles from Lottie as he talked throughout, putting her at ease. Isobel, however, fidgeted with her sticker, all her energies focused on pushing that forgotten dream of a big family to the dark recesses of her mind. Why had that idea come to her now after being buried for so long?

She suspected it was because this time, the new babies in that old fantasy looked an awful lot like Cash.

Chapter Eight

Cash stuck his head into the freezer, more for the cooling blast than to search for a midnight snack. He'd only managed to sleep for a couple of hours before the nightmares kicked in, leaving his brain and nerves on fire as if he were right back in the flames that stole his friend's life.

Except tonight his dreams differed from the standard replay of that fatal accident. The past tangled up with the present. Instead of a blaze in Montana, his sleep had filled with torturous images of the Moonlight Ridge library burning to the ground, books igniting, digital archives melting. He'd struggled to push his way through, one moment in full firefighter gear. Then the next in just jeans and a T-shirt. Except once he'd pushed his way past a flaming bookshelf, he found Isobel and Lottie rather than his friend. And even in the fugue-like state, Cash knew he wouldn't be able to save them any more than he'd rescued Elijah.

Dreams were brutal beasts. He was better off abandoning sleep.

Slamming the freezer closed, he opened the refrigerator side with the other. He bypassed a craft brew for a bottled water. The last thing he needed was to medicate his nightmares with alcohol.

His hand skimmed behind his neck, rubbing along the ridged scar tissue. He shook his head clear and drained half the water bottle before setting it aside on the counter.

Without the refrigerator light, darkness shrouded the room in a depressing cloud, but he didn't want to risk waking the others by flicking on a bunch of lights. Maybe he should take a midnight jog? Clear his head. Keep the focus on maintaining his recovery from the injuries. He was already wearing jogging shorts and a T-shirt, his modest nightwear since he'd been sharing the cabin with Isobel and Lottie.

After lacing up his gym shoes, he reached for the doorknob, only to find it unlocked. Protective urges went on alert. As a firefighter he saw his fair share of violence, enough to put a dent in his trust in mankind at times.

He weighed whether to check inside or out, where he might find a weapon, until he peered deeper in the yard… Isobel.

Moonbeams streamed down on her as she sat by the firepit, her computer on her lap as she typed away. Did bad dreams keep her awake as well? Or was she simply this overworked?

Needing to do something to ease her load, Cash made a quick return trip to the refrigerator for a second water bottle and jogged outside again. Not to the running trail. Instead, he made a beeline for Isobel.

Her dark hair trailed over the back of the Adirondack chair. The fire crackled lowly, the mountain nights chilly even in the summer. Had a hint of the smoke from the blaze filtered through his windows and ignited the nightmare? Not that it took much these days.

The firelight played over Isobel's face, revealing her intent expression while her fingers flew over the keys. Her legs were bare in sleep shorts, and she'd pulled on her favorite sweatshirt. He wondered what else she wore underneath.

He leaned on the back of the empty Adirondack next to her. "Careful or you'll melt the soles of your slippers."

She bolted upright, slamming her feet to the ground and scuffing them in the dirt. "Oh man, I was so caught up in work, I'm not sure I would have even noticed."

He passed her the unopened water bottle. "Here, I thought you might want this. Don't let me stop you though. I don't want to disrupt your work time."

Even though he hated the idea of her forsaking sleep for her job.

She smiled with gratitude. "I'm at a good stopping point if you want to join me." She took the bottle and twisted the cap. "Thanks for this. The smoky air has left me a little parched. Nothing compared to what you experience at work though."

He didn't want to talk about work. Especially not with the nightmare still chasing around his brain. He dropped another log on the fire before sinking into the Adirondack chair beside her. "That was wild seeing the photograph of your grandmother during story time."

A night bird called overhead, the yard quiet except for the occasional snap and pop of the fire.

"Quite serendipitous." She closed her laptop and tucked it under her chair. "If only there'd been a family tree conveniently attached."

"We'll get there. The donor drive is only a little over a week away." And after that? He would leave for his new hometown at a different station. A fresh start. No emotional entanglements. "Maybe I could come back for a visit when Lottie has her surgery."

"Maybe," she said, noncommittally. "We would love to see you, but please don't feel obligated. You'll probably be all caught up in putting down roots."

He couldn't tell if she was brushing him off or offering him a graceful out. Better to let the subject drop. "Have you given any more thought to taking some time for yourself while you're here?"

Her cheeks puffed with a hefty exhale as she drew her legs up to hug them to her chest. "It's tough to think of anything other than finding a match for Lottie. Maybe after that, I can take the Top Dog brochure and make a list for myself."

"Be sure to send me pictures of you two living your best life." He stuffed down the twinge of regret that he wouldn't be there to see it.

"Sure," she said with a smile. Another brush-off? "How was your horseback outing today?"

"Fun. Relaxing. It's been a while, but I remembered more than I thought."

"I didn't know you ride." She scratched a fingernail

along the rough wooden arm of her oak chair. "I guess there's a lot we haven't shared."

True enough. He'd been so intent on making sure to keep things light so it would be easier to walk away. But he wanted to know more about her. And he suspected he wouldn't pry anything free unless he shared something of his own.

He searched her face for a moment before saying, "Dad worked on a ranch for a while—odd jobs for extra money. He would take me with him whenever mom was pulling an additional shift. As a perk, we got to trail-ride at no cost."

"Your dad sounds very involved."

"He was. He had to be, really." His parents had to make tough choices to care for him, but they both had stepped up. He was lucky. He missed them and the sense of family he'd had growing up. "Mom made more in her job as a nurse than he did working construction, so her career was the primary income. Would he have done so much otherwise? I like to think so. But in the end, what does it matter either way?"

A frown flitted across her forehead, and her gaze slid away. She hugged her legs closer, night bugs humming in the silence between them.

He leaned forward in his seat, elbows on his knees. "Did I say something wrong?"

She shook her head. "Not at all." Her bluish-green eyes filled with unmistakable sadness as they met his. "I was just wondering if Colin would have been more involved with Lottie if he worked a regular nine-to-five."

Not for the first time, Cash wondered about her ex. In the past six months, his path had never crossed with the guy. Which seemed odd then and now. The guy had missed out on a lot. "He's a truck driver, right?"

"Right. He had easier hours right after she was born, and I told myself he would be more active in her life when she was older. Some men just don't get the baby thing," she said wryly. "Then he started taking on long-haul drives because we needed the extra money. Face-Time isn't the same as being there in person."

There wasn't any safe answer to give. If he tore apart Colin's absence, then he would be insulting Lottie's father. But Cash sure didn't feel like defending the guy. From everything he'd seen, the man looked for every excuse possible to dodge tougher responsibilities. And Isobel made excuses.

He got in late from a trip. He needs to sleep in.

Time zones messed with his schedule, so he couldn't call.

He had a cold, so best not to take Lottie for her checkup.

And right now, Cash worried if he heard another of those excuses, he would spout off about the guy, which would probably only make the tension on Isobel's forehead trench deeper.

He rolled the plastic bottle between his palms. "I have a challenge for you."

Her face cleared at the change of subject. "That sounds…interesting?"

"Hear me out." He rested a hand on her knee. Her oh-so-soft knee. His hand gripped a hint tighter. "What do you say we each choose an event here at the ranch and go together?"

"Like a date?" She winced.

A date? Maybe. No. He didn't know what to call it. He just knew he needed for her to say yes. "A date would be if we went downtown out to dinner. This is just two friends making the most of our time at the ranch."

The feel of her skin beneath his fingers made him question why he was insisting on the "just friends" angle.

"If—and I do mean *if*—we were to enter this challenge, what about Lottie?" More of that tension creased her face. "Who would watch her?"

He'd actually given that some thought after noticing the other parents on outings. "The ranch has sitter services, and plenty of parents leave their kids at the different pack-tivities."

"A stranger? Who may or may not understand Lottie's medical needs?" She bit her lip.

"No pressure." He linked a hand with hers, his thumb stroking the inside of her wrist. "It's just a suggestion, if you were to find someone you trust to watch Lottie. You don't have to answer now."

She scrunched her nose for a moment. "I'll think about it."

Briefly forgetting himself, he lifted their clasped hands and kissed her fingers. She gasped. But she didn't pull away. The space between them crackled like lightning bugs electrifying the air. A rush of desire seeped through his veins, the barely banked attraction flaring to life.

He angled closer, hesitated, waiting for her to make the next move. His pulse hammered in his ears, pounding away seconds for what must have been a full minute. Just as he began to give up hope, her legs slid to the ground and she pressed her lips to his.

A sigh passed between them, her breath or his. Maybe both. Then as quickly as the kiss began, it ended as she angled away. Their connection so brief that he half wondered if he'd dreamt it.

Except even his dreams never felt that good, that real.

She licked her lips before saying, "I don't mean to state the obvious, but we just kissed. And it wasn't a 'friend' kind."

He should have known she would address the impulsive moment head-on.

"Friends with benefits?" When her eyes went wide, he rushed to add, "Scratch that. We both got carried away. It won't happen again. Our friendship is too valuable to risk."

And he meant that. But he also couldn't bring himself to regret kissing her.

"I agree," she said with a finality that signaled the conversation was over. "We need to protect the friendship."

He certainly didn't want to hash this out further, not with his brain still so scrambled from one simple kiss. He shoved to his feet. "I'm going for a run. I hope you'll think over the suggestion for outings before I leave. You deserve the chance to have some fun, Isobel."

Pivoting away from the sight of her all mussed and

inviting, he set off onto the hiking path. Every hammering footstep along the dusty earth reminding him he couldn't outrace the attraction any more than the nightmares.

Isobel was on her second scoop of Rocky Road and seriously foresaw a third in her future. Lottie had chosen a late morning pack-tivity at the Bone Appétit Café, churning ice cream and making dog treats.

Stirring her spoon through the paper cup, she scooped up another blob and let the creamy taste melt through her senses that were already on high alert since Cash's kiss last night. After he left—his "friends with benefits" comment still hanging in the air—she hadn't been able to work or sleep.

So, now, here she sat at a little iron parlor table in a far corner of the café. Her laptop cursor blinked on a blank page as she ate her body weight in ice cream, wondering where things stood with Cash. At least Lottie was having a blast, unaware of the tensions as she rolled out dough for dog biscuits along with her new friends. Hollie O'Brien moved smoothly from child to child, helping them press out shapes and take turns cranking the churn.

Scents of cinnamon and vanilla clung to the space filled with wrought iron tables and chairs on the patio as well as inside. There were two sides to the shop, one with human treats and one with pooch treats. Ice cream. Cakes. Cookies.

The dogs around here got treats too—pup-sicles and pup-cakes. Apparently, this was Hollie's domain, and she had definitely managed to blend her culinary background with her spouse's animal husbandry training. This would make a fun setting for Isobel's next blog…

The bells over the door chimed, giving her only a moment's warning before Zelda's voice carried across the room.

Zelda waved enthusiastically. "Yoo-hoo. Isobel, look who drove through the night to see us early."

Close behind trailed Neve—such a welcome sight. Although she didn't look like someone who'd driven straight over after closing her college office for the sabbatical. Her dark hair fell perfectly to her shoulders, her yellow slacks and blue silk shirt wrinkle free as if she had just started her day.

Isobel shot to her feet and wrapped her sister in a hug for the first time since Gran's funeral.

Zelda joined to wrap her arms around them both for a hard squeeze before stepping back. "Let's sit so these folks can enjoy their ice cream in peace. I'll get orders in while you two talk."

As Zelda leaned over the ice cream counter, Isobel motioned Neve to her table in the far corner. "I can't believe you're really here," Isobel said, shuffling her things to the side to make room for her sisters. "I'm sorry I wasn't there to greet you when you arrived."

Neve brushed aside the apology. "I'm the one who's early. Lottie's in the middle of a craft. Joining you at an ice cream parlor was an easy decision."

"How was the drive? You must be tired." Isobel was certainly exhausted from lack of sleep and she wasn't behind the wheel.

"Not at all." Neve adjusted her pearl earring while she took in the café, her eyes darting from one end of the room to the other. "I decided it would be more efficient to drive through the night. And what do you know? I timed it just right to avoid traffic."

Of course she did. Neve was the queen of spin. Everything was better than great, more like fantastic, no trouble at all. And while nobody liked a whiner, Neve's over-the-top optimism could be exhausting to match. Sometimes Isobel wanted to shake her and beg her to be *real*.

But that wouldn't accomplish anything other than sending Neve flitting away. "I'm glad. You know my phobia of mountain roads, so the trip was a bit more laborious for me."

There. She'd shared a vulnerability in the interest of being authentic.

"Well," Zelda interjected, setting a tray on the table with ice cream and three cups of coffee, "I got a speeding ticket on my trip here."

Zelda shot a quick wink at Isobel.

Neve blew into her coffee, unfazed. "You should try cruise control, Zelda. Seriously. But once I heard about that picture of Gran, I just couldn't wait another minute to be here. Have you found out anything more about the image?"

Isobel spooned sugar into her java. "From what I could piece together from the internet, it was from a school field trip. Most of the others in the photos were in Gran's class, and we've got their names. But there's one—a teenage boy—we can't track down. Next, I'll move to phoning others in the photo."

Zelda dabbed strawberry ice cream from the corner of her mouth. "We don't know if he's from another school locally or if he was a tourist. It's not much to go on, but it's a start."

Neve gave a brisk nod, indicating the information had been stored away for examination later. "How's Lottie's health? How much time do we have?"

Isobel's shoulders slumped. She hated questions like this—ones without a definitive answer. "We've met with her new GP and he's a sharp doctor. He's keeping an eagle eye on her lab work to monitor her kidney function. We're safe for now, but…"

Zelda squeezed her forearm. "He sounds committed to helping her. And we *are* going to find a donor here." Isobel breathed deep, allowing herself to soak up the moment of comfort. Just having both her sisters here by her side, was…well, amazing. She hadn't known how much she needed them for this journey, but considering the dark moments of panic she'd been feeling lately, she really did need the moral support.

Neve settled her coffee mug back on the iron tabletop, spinning the handle to a precise angle before adding, "Zel and I were talking on the phone during my drive, and we want you to be rested and refreshed going into the surgery. You need to pace yourself."

Ugh. They sounded like Dr. Barnett. And why did she bristle a little when realizing she'd been the topic of a sister discussion? She knew they meant well. "I am. Thank you."

Zelda tutted. "That's up for debate, but let's put that aside. We would really love it if you would let us watch Lottie so you can have some downtime. I know she has health concerns and that may make it tougher for you to leave her. But we're here and we've missed spending time with her. If you're concerned, stay close, here on the ranch."

Their offer sounded enticing, but Lottie was her responsibility. And her joy. "Thank you, but I don't want to take advantage. You both have lives and your work—"

Neve cut her off short. "After teaching at the same time I was finishing my PhD, this work-study sabbatical will be a cakewalk."

And she could probably do it all standing on her head.

The uncharitable thought made Isobel feel guilty. Neve was making a generous offer.

Zelda continued, "It's easy for me to swap shifts. The other groomers already owe me for filling in at the last minute. Come on. Mull it over."

Tapping her fingernails against her ceramic mug, Isobel let the offer sift in her head. Cash had mentioned wanting to take turns choosing an outing here at the ranch. This would give her the perfect opening. Not that she wanted a repeat of the kiss.

But maybe she really could use some time to recharge her batteries before the next phase of Lottie's journey. "Are you really sure? It's okay to back out."

Her sisters whooped and high-fived each other across the table before Zelda settled back into her seat. "Not another word. Consider it a done deal."

* * *

When Zelda volunteered to take Lottie on an outing, she definitely hadn't counted on her niece choosing equine therapy with rodeo hotshot, Troy Shaw.

At least, so far, he was nowhere in sight in the stable yard. A split rail fence sectioned off a corral for the young riders. Top Dog staff guided the children on ponies and small horses in a circle, one person with each rider. Even her understandably protective sister would approve.

Zelda snapped a photo of Lottie on a Shetland pony with flowers woven into the mane. The adaptive saddle steadied her on either side, her pink cowgirl hat perched on her head with pride.

Tucking her cell into her back pocket, Zelda reclaimed her Yeti full of dark roast from the ground by her feet. Her new cowgirl boots were pinching her toes, but she intended to get use out of the overpriced purchase she really couldn't afford, especially since she spent most of the day in rubber boots washing dogs.

Neve had wandered off to check out the petting zoo under the auspices of finding the gentlest creatures to meet Lottie. Zelda knew Neve really just wanted an excuse to hang out with the animals. Growing up, she would wander in the woods for hours, often returning with a wounded creature.

"Hey, beautiful," a deep voice rumbled from behind her an instant before Troy pulled up beside her to lean a lazy hip against the fence post. "How was your day washing pooches?"

Her shoulders tensed, and she cut a sideways glance

at him, trying not to notice his long legs in crisp denim. "I think you're paying me a compliment, but saying something nice about a person's looks isn't really saying much of substance. Appearance is beyond our control."

She was quite proud of her speech, given her tongue threatened to stick to the roof of her mouth like she'd eaten peanut butter with nothing to drink. She hated, hated, hated that her ex had left her with these insecurities around men.

"Fair enough." He knuckled his Stetson up, revealing a hint of dark hair. "So, is your sister some kind of Dr. Doolittle?"

Zelda startled. "What do you mean?"

"Your sister, over there." He gestured toward the pig pen, where Neve crouched and talked between the slats. "She's been chattering away to all the animals in the barn this morning."

Was he interested in her sister? Well, Neve was welcome to him. "Oh, yes, she's a wildlife biologist. She's always preferred critters to people."

A half smile kicked a dimple into one tanned cheek. "I can't say that I blame her."

She pivoted to face him full on. "Do I take that to mean you're interested? Because if you're looking for me to supply the inside track on my own flesh and blood for some rodeo stud, then you're sadly mistaken."

He turned up the grin to full wattage. "You think I'm a stud?"

Oh heavens. She rolled her eyes. "I think you're insufferable."

Neve would shut him down in three seconds flat.

"But you're not walking away."

"Oh, I can rectify that." She hugged her Yeti to her chest and started walking. She didn't know where she was going since she'd promised to keep Lottie within eyesight. But her sore, booted feet were moving.

"Hey," Troy called out, "hold up." He jogged across the arena, catching up in a half dozen long strides.

Stopping in her tracks, she hitched her hands on her hips. "Clearly I did not deflate your overblown ego enough if you're back for more."

"I apologize." He swept off his Stetson, smacking it against the side of his leg. "I thought we were…uh… bantering?"

He wasn't wrong. And from the looks of things, he wasn't interested in Neve after all.

Zelda sighed. "I'm not a buckle bunny looking for a hookup."

"I don't recall asking you," he said with a quirked eyebrow.

"Oh." She wasn't speechless often. She didn't like what that said about his appeal.

"Right. We're both new here at the ranch." He searched the sky as if looking for the right words before he swiped an arm across his forehead and plunked his hat in place again. "I was making conversation, and yes, I fell into old habits. I apologize for stepping out of line. I'll try to do better going forward."

Was he genuine? Or a player? She didn't know and it honestly didn't matter. Because even if her boots weren't made for walking, the last thing she needed was even a hint of a romantic entanglement. "Apology accepted. Now don't let me keep you from work."

She turned her attention back to Lottie and made a beeline in her niece's direction. And with every painful step, she reminded herself that blisters on her heels weren't nearly as painful as the ones on her heart.

Chapter Nine

Cash never thought he would participate in a baby goat yoga class, much less initiate attending. But when choosing a pack-tivity for Isobel, he'd known this fit the bill. A mix of fun and relaxation, tying into her love for animals.

Of course, he hadn't envisioned himself on all fours with a goat on his back. Still, it was centering in a strange way he hadn't anticipated.

The late morning sun cast a mellow glow over the stream. Fish jumped and plopped, the water rippling over rocks, widening to a river about fifty yards away. Thank goodness Zelda and Neve had stepped up with the offer to watch Lottie for equine therapy and lunch. Although Isobel had texted for updates every five minutes until the session began.

The yoga master knelt on a purple mat by the shore. A guitarist from the Raise the Woof band sat cross-legged in the grass plucking out classical tunes. Arching and relaxing her spine, the instructor chanted, "Cat, cow, cat, cow."

Easier said than done. Cash's balance was shaky due to a cramp threatening in his thigh until he was about to cat, cow, catapult his four-legged passenger—aka Lucy—into the river. He shot his arm behind him, palming the little goat.

Beside him, Isobel stifled giggles, her furry yoga partner curled up asleep between her shoulder blades. She had this Zen thing down pat.

He quirked an eyebrow and whispered, "Go ahead and chuckle. I'll be glad to trade with you. This one needs a serious pedicure."

She dissolved into laughter, waking the little one on her back. The startled critter hopped off and kicked up turf until a newlywed couple in front of them launched killer scowls.

Luckily, the instructor shifted positions, crooning, "Cobra pose..."

As Isobel settled her kid into place again, amusement sparkled in her eyes, glittering like the sun on the water. So much so, Cash missed the next call by the instructor. He refocused on shifting his pose without losing Lucy. Success. He'd enjoyed surprising Isobel with his choice. She'd been so certain he would select a rowdy outing—like whitewater rafting or hiking to a waterfall. Not that he would have ever chosen anything remotely related to her fear of heights. Yoga by the stream made perfect sense.

The ground was a soft carpet of lush grass, trees creating a barrier from the rest of the world. Utterly peaceful.

Well, other than the sight of Isobel in leggings and a fitted tank top. He would need a lot more than yoga to settle his heart rate. Her hair was gathered in a high ponytail, no make-up, totally gorgeous.

Was this what she looked like every morning? A wayward and too tempting thought at odds with the friendly outing he'd promised her.

"Ladies and gentlemen," the instructor interrupted his thoughts in a voice not much louder than the gurgle of the stream, "that concludes our session for today. Take your time coming out of your final pose. And feel free to play with your adorable goat."

Five deep breaths later, Cash opened his eyes again. He wasn't ready for this morning to end.

Isobel eased her baby goat to the ground, where the critter promptly began chomping the lawn alongside Lucy. "I can't believe that this was your choice for an outing."

"I'll have you know that yoga and Pilates require athleticism," he said proudly. "I did my research."

"Really?" She plucked at blades of grass, seemingly in no hurry to pack up and leave either. "How did I not know you're into Pilates?"

"I wasn't." He stroked aside a stray lock of her hair that had escaped her ponytail and tucked it behind her ear. "But I am into making you smile."

"Aww," she said with a snap of her fingers. "Now I know. You saw the flyer on the kitchen counter where I circled this event."

He winked, rubbing his palms together as if to capture the sensation of that lock against his skin. "I may have. But I confess that I'm enjoying it. I could have used stretches like this during PT. This is far more relaxing than the contortions my trainer put me through."

Her hand rested ever so lightly on his scarred leg, just above the skin graft. "You made a remarkable recovery."

Even the brief mention of that time sent his mind right back there to that awful day. The last place he wanted to be. He placed his hand over hers. "I don't want to talk about the accident today." He kept their fingers linked, connected, so natural. "Do you realize that in the past, we always had Lottie along? This is our first outing with only the two of us."

"I'm aware." She smiled but eased her hand away, glancing nervously at the others rolling up their mats. "I'm thankful for how kind you've been to my daugh—"

"Whoa, hold on. Don't misunderstand." He hated that his words had been misconstrued. "I adore Lottie, and I enjoy the time the three of us have spent together. I was merely commenting."

She searched his face with her eyes for so long he thought she would argue. Finally, she nodded.

"Okay, and in case you were wondering—" she grinned and stroked the goat nudging at her elbow "—I'm enjoying our time today too."

Cash scrubbed a hand along his jaw, stubbled since he'd skipped his shave this morning. Soon enough, he would be back at work, shaving regularly. Might as well make the most of it. "I have to admit this one was a bit outside my comfort zone with the addition of live goats, but I really enjoyed it."

Hearing Isobel's laugh had made the experience all the more special.

"I'm glad." When her goat wandered away to rejoin the others wading into the water, Isobel leaned back on her hands, her shirt stretching tighter across the gentle curves of her breasts. "Thank you again for the whole idea to select outings for each other."

As he took in the sight of her looking so relaxed and at peace, he wondered—not for the first time—about the man who wasn't here. Her ex-husband. Lottie's father.

The drive to know more about the guy was stronger now, for whatever reason, and Cash couldn't stop the question he'd held in for months. "What's the deal with Lottie's dad? I can't recall having the opportunity to meet him."

She blinked quickly at the subject change, fidgeting, scrunching her toes until the joints popped. "He's a truck driver for a major grocery store chain. He's on the road a lot, but Lottie needs the health insurance."

He'd heard the part about needing the insurance before, but the part about her ex's employer was new.

Then he realized what he really wanted to know. What he needed to know. He didn't bother questioning why. "Do you still love him?"

Once the question was out there between them, he expected her to tell him he was nosy. That it was none of his business. Or even worse that, yes, she still yearned to have the guy back in her life.

"No, not anymore," she said, meeting his gaze dead-on with complete honesty and a hint of regret. "He may be a decent dad, but he wasn't a decent husband. He cheated while away, often. I think if I hadn't found out, we'd still be married today, and that hurts to even think about. Being so delusional, so gullible."

Her jaw jutted but trembled.

Cash bit back the urge to curse over the pain he'd brought with his intrusive question. So he kept his voice level, or at least tried. "You're an honest person, and you should have been able to take your husband at his word."

"Yes, I should have." A deep breath later, she waved a hand and plastered on an overbright smile. "But enough of that. We're supposed to be relaxing."

And he could see the subject was far from tranquil for her. He needed to stay focused on his plan for the outings, no more detouring into complicated waters about the past.

"You're absolutely correct," he said, relieved to know she wasn't still pining for her ex-husband. Far more relieved than he ought to be, considering he didn't plan to romance her when he was leaving soon anyhow. "So, what do you have planned for me tomorrow?"

Isobel's eyes lit with a mischievous gleam as she pushed to her feet, dusting off her too cute bottom. "You'll just have to wait and see, won't you?"

And that's how I found out downward-facing dog wasn't a sad puppy.
Baaaaa-maste.

Sitting at the kitchen island, Isobel clicked Save, then closed her laptop with a huge sigh of relief that she'd managed to finish before her daughter returned from lunch with her aunts. Another blog complete, this one about baby goat yoga, even if Cocoa technically hadn't been present. Isobel tried not to think of how often her topics were inspired by Cash lately.

She had a serious case of the munchies, which surely had nothing to do with wishing her time with Cash this morning could have lasted longer. She slid from the barstool and tugged open the pantry door, searching for a snack that would qualify as a meal.

The two hours of quiet after yoga had been incredibly productive. She wondered sometimes what she could accomplish with a regular eight-hour workday in one place focused on just her job. But then she would miss out on priceless memories with her daughter, like the pirate tea party.

And, man, there her thoughts had gone right back to Cash again.

The sound of footsteps and female voices outside on the porch gave her a moment's notice to haul her focus right back on the present and her family. The photos her sisters had texted of Lottie on the pony, followed by a hot dog cookout, showed she'd had the best time. She would nap well this afternoon before they drove into town for Lottie's appointment at her new PT facility.

The door swung wide as Zelda strode inside carrying a sack from the Top Dog gift shop. "Sorry, we ran a little late, but we needed some merch." She tossed the bag onto the leather sofa. "How was the yoga?"

Behind her, Neve pushed Lottie's chair, Cocoa in step. "How was Cash this morning?"

Zelda winked. "Was he suitably impressed with your *flexibility*?"

"Shhh." Isobel glared at her sisters and knelt in front of her daughter, who was drifting off to sleep. Apparently, Lottie hadn't missed her at all and was too worn out to talk now.

"What?" Zelda called after Isobel as she took her daughter to her room for a nap. That didn't stop her sister from talking though. "I'm only expressing interest in your morning of exercising."

Isobel knew she meant well and it was all good-natured teasing, but her heart was still tender from the combination of Cash at his most charming followed by talk of her ex.

Cash's question had surprised her. Throughout their friendship, they'd been careful to respect unspoken boundaries. Like not asking much about romantic relationships. Yet Cash had waded right into a discussion of her failed marriage, and she had to ask herself…why?

Once she had her daughter and Cocoa settled for a nap, she took an extra few seconds to gather her composure before walking back into the living area. "We had a lovely time. It was very peaceful by the stream. And the baby goats were adorable. I got some great photos for my next blog."

"Uh-huh." Zelda slung her backpack into an over-stuffed leather chair. "You're looking mighty flushed from your peaceful afternoon. Makes me wonder what will happen at your next adventure with the hunky firefighter."

Isobel clenched her fists at her side to keep her

hands from flying to her face. "I appreciate the help this morning, but I gotta know—am I going to get the third degree again if I go somewhere else with Cash?"

Because she still had her turn choosing an outing, and she truly was looking forward to seeing his face when she told him.

Neve slid an arm around her shoulders and gave her a quick, side hug. "We're just excited you're having fun. Please don't let our silliness stop you. We're just teasing you."

"I know you mean well," Isobel said, sinking to a barstool at the island, "and that you care about me. It's just that Cash is leaving in another week, and he's starting a new job in a new town. We were friends before we got here and that isn't going to change. Okay?"

She kept telling herself as much, anyway. Even if the dynamics between them seemed to have shifted since they'd arrived at Top Dog.

Zelda slid onto the seat beside her, fidgeting with ceramic salt and pepper shakers shaped like black bears. "So, what *are* you planning to do for your next outing together?"

Isobel flattened her hands to the butcher block counter and let her excitement bubble free. She had put a lot of thought into her choice. "We're going whitewater rafting."

Zelda's eyes went wide. The bears toppled over, spilling salt and pepper. "You? Whitewater rafting? You get seasick on a merry-go-round."

Neve tutted, sitting on her other side and folding her hands in her lap. "Remember when Gran took us to that little county fair after we'd gone shopping for school clothes?"

Zelda scrunched her sunburned nose. "We rode the Ferris wheel and you barfed on my new sandals."

Great. Talk about putting a damper on her plan. She'd been so proud of herself for stepping outside her comfort zone. She folded her arms over her chest. "I'm not feeling the sisterly love in this story."

Neve tapped the countertop for emphasis, her best professor face in place. "My point is you were mostly upset because the guy running the ride was cute. You were *mortified*."

True. Isobel righted the salt and pepper shakers. "I remember the event well. But thanks for reminding me."

Zelda shrugged. "Just seems to me you wouldn't want Cash to see you hurl."

"I'm not thirteen anymore," Isobel reminded them gently. Maybe reminding herself as well. "I'm broadening my horizons. Trying new things. Maybe I'll love it."

Why did her voice sound weak even to her own ears? She really did want to make the effort for Cash. He deserved a fun memory before he left, and she wanted to be a part of that. He'd been so good to her, and Lottie too.

"Okay then," Neve said, sweeping her hand across the loose salt and pepper and catching it in her other palm. "But you do realize that if you hate it, there's no getting out of the boat early?"

Ever the know-it-all.

Isobel ground her teeth for three seconds before venturing an answer. "Of course I know that. I'll take Dramamine. It'll be fine."

Now even Zelda gave her a skeptical look. "And if it's not?"

"I guess I'll just throw up in the water," Isobel said wryly before standing. "But thanks for worrying. And for helping with Lottie today."

She knew they only asked questions about Cash because they cared. There was no need to feel so defensive. But then again, she had to wonder if she was trying to convince them...

Or herself.

The next day, Cash shuffled from foot to foot in the cabin living room, feeling like a teenager waiting for his date. But instead of an overbearing father, it was a sister eyeing him with undisguised curiosity—and protectiveness.

At least Zelda wasn't grilling him about his intentions. And Neve hadn't arrived yet.

Zelda stood behind Lottie, brushing the child's hair into a ponytail. "Do you have a guess about what Isobel chose for your outing this morning?"

Was that humor in her quickly averted eyes?

Hmmm. Dropping to the sofa, he tugged on his gym shoes. "Well, since she told me to dress in swim trunks, my first guess is that we're going to the hot springs."

Lottie's hand shot up in the air. "I know, I know. I know where you're going. Mommy told me—"

Zelda angled down. "Shhh. It's a surprise." She looked back up at Cash. "And your second guess?"

"Canoeing?" he asked hopefully. He could envision Isobel lounging in the front of the boat in her swimsuit while he rowed them into a private cove—

From the smirks exchanged by Zelda and her niece, he must have missed the mark. He thought through the rest of the ranch's pack-tivities...pottery making, art therapy, square dancing.

Flower arranging?

Standing, he crossed to the kitchen and washed his hands before leaning a hip against the counter, snagging a molasses cookie. Lottie had been proud of the dozen she baked at the Bone Appétit Café. He could get used to the incredible food around this place. "What do you have on tap for Lottie today?"

Lottie squealed, her ponytail swishing. "Horses again this morning. That's my most favorite."

Zelda's smile went tight as she gathered up the brush along with the extra rubber bands and bows. "It's in the arena today. Troy Shaw will be showing off some of his champion rodeo moves."

Nodding, Lottie wheeled her chair into a turn to face Cash. "Then Aunt Neve is taking me to archery. Maybe that'll be my new favorite. I've never tried it before. I hope I hit the target."

Zelda adjusted Cocoa's service dog vest. "We split shifts today since I need to work this afternoon."

"Thanks for making it possible." He dusted the crumbs off his fingers. "Isobel's a tough one to convince to take time for herself."

"Don't we always work to be different from our parents?" Zelda said with a wistful air. "So convinced we won't make their mistakes."

"I'm not following." But he wasn't going to pass up the insight into Isobel. He was only just coming to realize how little of herself she'd shared over the past six months.

Or maybe he'd been too self-absorbed in his own pain to take note of hers. He didn't like what that said about him.

Zelda paused for a moment as Lottie rolled across the room with Cocoa, chattering softly to her dog about their day ahead. Zelda returned her attention to Cash. "Our parents were incredible people with a heart for service. They devoted their lives to teaching in underserved communities and overseas."

Sounded admirable. Although he sensed a catch, reservation in her tone. "But…?"

"They didn't have a lot of time or energy left for their own kids," she said, her shrug sad but resigned as she joined him at the kitchen sink. "That's why Gran was such an important part of our lives. We stayed with her often."

"Isobel has spoken fondly of those summer vacations." He'd thought her parents joined in too. Apparently not.

"Gran is the one who gave us roots, a place to call home as our parents moved from one job to the next." Zelda rushed to add, "I don't mean to sound ungrateful. Mom and Dad loved us and instilled a thirst for knowledge."

"I've noticed that in Isobel." He enjoyed seeing what

she came up with next for her blog. Her creativity had impressed him from the start. He'd assumed it came from her grandmother's storytelling.

Zelda shot a quick glance at the empty hall before leaning forward to whisper, "I just want to help you understand why Isobel pushes herself so very hard. She's insistent on being present for Lottie—which is admirable, no question—but I worry about her and hate that I can't help more."

"You live far away," he said, even though he'd wished the same thing for Isobel. "And she's told me about her ex and the necessity of his insurance."

Zelda shook her head, again checking the hall and then Lottie as well, keeping her voice low as she blurted, "Her ex is a jerk who keeps taking whatever jobs will keep him on the road the most so he doesn't have to parent Lottie." Mouth tight, she crossed her arms over her chest. "There. I said it."

He was Team Zelda when it came to defending Isobel.

Finally, he let himself ask the question that had been dogging him for months, and yes, even though he'd asked Isobel, he wasn't sure he trusted her answer. "Does she still have feelings for him?"

"Not so far as I can tell," Zelda said, chewing her thumbnail and looking less than confident in her answer. "It seems to go back to trying to create the perfect family for Lottie."

Cash couldn't ignore the hopeful relief at hearing further confirmation that Isobel wasn't carrying a torch for her former husband. "Seems obvious to me that Lottie already has the perfect mother."

"Awww," Isobel crooned from the hallway. How long had she been standing there? "Thank you so much…"

She may have said something more after that, but the sight of her in a sheer cover-up, her sleek black swimsuit underneath showcasing subtle curves, stole the breath from his lungs. He didn't know yet where they were headed, but right now, he did know he would follow her off the edge of the universe just to keep soaking up the tempting sight of her.

Chapter Ten

Troy's dating hiatus was being seriously challenged by the seemingly never-ending, tempting glimpses of Zelda Dawson.

And here she was again, like a bad sexy penny turning up in the ranch's small arena. Even though he'd seen her yesterday during the equine therapy session. Was she seeking him out? Tough to imagine, considering the ways she'd shut him down up until now. But if she'd somehow changed her mind about him, he would need to make it clear he wouldn't—couldn't—act on the attraction.

Hauling his attention off her long legs in fitted jeans, he focused on last-minute touches for today's class featuring scaled-down rodeo moves. He drew in bracing breaths, the scent of hay and earth like a heady perfume.

The ranch's arena had been a pleasant surprise when he'd accepted this summer gig. Sure, the ranch had an impressive spread of barns and stables, but this space offered a superb option for events, like today's faux rodeo for the little ones. A half dozen kids were clustered in a far corner taking turns giving a bottle to a calf, simple country tunes playing over the sound system. Another section sported craft tables for making their own rodeo puppets for a show later.

He made a final adjustment to a barrel strategically placed. Then another. And, yes, his boots were carrying him closer to Zelda as she fed a carrot to one of the ponies in the corner corral.

The lady had style, he had to admit. From a purely objective perspective. Even in her Top Dog tee and her pink galoshes—no cowgirl boots today—she'd woven flowers through her long braid. Every little pink posy called to his fingers to unravel that plait.

Sure, he should walk away. And he would. Soon. "What brings you here again today? I thought you worked in the grooming salon?"

She offered the last of the carrot to the Shetland before turning to face him. "I do, but my shift starts later today." The pony rested its head on her shoulder. She stroked the muzzle. "I'm here with my niece so my other sister can go whitewater rafting with her friend. Apparently, your class is Lottie's favorite."

From the scowl on Zelda's face, she didn't appear happy about her niece's choice. Not in the least. *Interesting.*

The urge to run eased. "That's nice of you, taking her to an event that's not your jam. Mind if I ask why you're not a fan? You're a natural with the pony."

"I have food. I think that's his only prerequisite for friendship," she said with a laugh. "I don't dislike horseback riding."

"So, it's me?" He clapped a hand to his chest.

She leaned closer to speak as latecomers, a mother

with two children, raced past to the class in the corner. "Some might call your obvious surprise rather arrogant."

"I've been called worse." He had the answer to his question. He should move on. Instead, he did the opposite by initiating more chitchat. "What's the deal with your sister and her friend? I heard he's leaving soon."

"Isobel and Cash are just friends," she explained as the pony whinnied behind her. "He just helped her with the drive here from Montana."

"Montana? Whew," he whistled softly, scuffing the toe of his boot across the dusty ground, confused and frustrated with himself that he couldn't seem to walk away from this woman. "All the way across country. That's a mighty big ask of a *friend*."

"From what I've seen of him, he's a good guy."

"And you're a good aunt to help. Having family to pitch in is a lifesaver for a single parent." He knew from experience. He was on his own raising Harper, and it was hard. Harder than he could have imagined.

Frowning, Zelda nibbled at her bottom lip. "Actually, I haven't been there for her as much as I should." Guilt clouded her eyes. "I feel bad. I got so wrapped up in my own problems that I let her down when she needed me most."

Something in her sad expression tugged at him. Or maybe it was her authenticity, a rare trait in a world that thrived on artifice and social influence. "You're here now. That means a lot."

Her gaze slid up to meet his, more of that sadness

lurking in her blue eyes. "You're a nice guy trying to make me feel better."

"Not that nice," he said, especially when his thoughts at the moment were filled with wanting to tangle up with this lady, to cajole a smile from her, chase away the shadows, "not really. I just call it as I see it."

"And what do you see?" she asked, not in a flirty or arrogant fashion, but more like...

She didn't know herself?

Without thinking, he rested his hands on her shoulders, the curves soft and fragile under his palms. "I see a woman with a big heart who's being too rough on herself—because of that big heart."

He waited for her to pull away, to put him in his place for saying something so personal to a woman he barely knew. What happened to his plan to send her running? As he stood here staring into her pretty eyes, he felt more off-kilter than in a bull-riding competition.

"Dad? Dad," his teenage daughter's voice startled him out of his idiotic haze. Talk about a proverbial falling to earth with a thud.

Troy cleared his throat and searched the arena until he located Harper stalking toward him, oozing defiance and bravado. Her most common attitude since her mother walked out. "Just a minute, Harper. I'll be right there."

Zelda blinked away the haze and stepped back. "I won't keep you."

"I'm sorry..." For what, he didn't know exactly.

But he did know for certain his daughter needed him and stability. Time to get his head on straight, focus on building a future for himself and Harper. He just had to get through this summer at the ranch to reshape his image and win over the financial backer crucial for launching a training facility.

Nothing—not even the sexiest dog groomer he'd ever met—could distract him.

Isobel walked backward along the path to the river, ahead of Cash so she could face him. She wanted to see every nuance of his reaction when he realized her plan for their outing. Twisted oaks shaded her path, the rustle of branches overhead mingling with the sound of rushing water in the distance. Deep green leaves decorated branches. White flowers on bushes lined their way like nature's guide.

Nerves skittered up her spine. Because of the impending rafting ride, of course, not because of the prospect of all afternoon with Cash.

"Are you ready for an adventure?" she asked, praying she hadn't taken on more than she could handle.

The raft.

The man.

"Absolutely." He ambled toward her, looking too yummy in his swim trunks and a T-shirt with the sleeves cut off. His backpack was slung over one shoulder. "And when are you going to tell me?"

"Soon. It's a surprise…" Was she holding back in telling him to give herself an escape in case she chickened out? The idea rankled her, so she stomped down any chance of letting herself off the hook. "We're going whitewater rafting."

His jaw dropped as he walked, speechless. The shock on his face delighted her. It was nice to knock him off balance for a change.

Then he smiled. "Ah, you're joking with me."

Turning, she slowed and fell into step alongside him, birds serenading their walk. "Not at all. I've always wanted to give it a try."

Well, *always* since the second day when they'd been walking with Lottie and she saw him eye one of the big rubber rafts afloat.

He gave a snort of disbelief. "You realize it's not a canoe ride, right?"

"I understand it makes our mountain trip seem like a leisurely Sunday drive." She hitched her beach bag higher onto her shoulder and swiped aside a spider web. "But I truly want to try it. It'll be more fun sharing the experience with you. Isn't that what you said about baby goat yoga?"

"You're right," he conceded, nudging a shoulder against hers. "Okay, I'm all in. But feel free to change your mind right up to the minute we're about to step into the raft."

"I won't," she insisted before confessing sheepishly, "I took Dramamine."

She'd taken the dose two hours ago, so hopefully it would have reached full effect once they launched. Because, yes, she did want the full experience.

"Ah, so it's not about a fear or phobia." He veered toward the right fork in the path, following the arrows posted to signs. His sneakers snapped twigs underfoot.

"If it's a medical issue causing the vertigo, why didn't you take the meds during our trip here?"

"Oh, I did." She kept extra in the glove compartment of her van. Then she realized what he must have assumed just now… "Please don't think I took advantage by having you drive out here. I can't drive when the meds are in my system. I get a little loopy and, over time, worry about an attack of vertigo starts to ramp the anxiety. It's a cycle."

"Loopy, huh?" He slowed his pace as they neared the clearing with a crowded dock in the distance. "I didn't notice."

"I'm not sure if that's a compliment. Do I act 'loopy' on a regular basis?" His words stung a bit. Sure she burned the candle at both ends, but she hated to appear disorganized around Cash. Could that be why he was so insistent on helping her? The sting doubled.

"No," he stopped, grasping her arm, "not at all. I'm sorry if that came out the wrong way. How's this for a compliment…? You're the most together—and hot—woman I know. In case you were wondering. And even if you weren't, I thought you should know."

A tingle started in her stomach, spreading through her veins. The heat had her eyeing the crystal-capped waters with longing.

His opinion shouldn't matter so much. But it did.

"Cash Warner, are you flirting with me?" She held her breath while waiting for him to answer.

"Maybe. A little." He paused just before a small wooden shack by the dock, stacks of rafts and canoes organized on metal racks. "They're not new thoughts. I've just never been able to share them before."

"What makes now different?" She hoped he had the answer, because heaven knew, she'd been searching for understanding of their changing feelings.

"Truthfully?" He shrugged. "Likely because I'm leaving soon."

"I don't understand." A stray breeze tickled her cheek, the warm mountain air fragrant with pine.

"Join the club," he said with a chuckle. "Let me re-phrase. It was easier to resist you in the past if I didn't say the words out loud. Keeping myself in check week after week. Month after month. Now, our time together is coming to a close. I just want you to hear—from me—what a captivating woman you are."

Surprise and pleasure stole the breath from her lungs, even as she recognized what he was saying. That he'd held back because they weren't ever going to be together as more than friends. And yet, she couldn't deny that his admission sent a thrill of awareness through her.

She wrestled with what to say, whether to compli-ment him back—easy enough to do. But she couldn't deny she wanted the flirting to last a little longer. To savor this easy moment between them without worry of the outside world. "Captivating? You're quite the poet today."

How much further would they take this? How far did she dare?

She was saved from answering by the arrival of a young couple hurrying down the path toward the water. They were both decked out in name-brand boating gear—from their personalized life jackets—Simon and Allegra—to their water shoes. The woman lifted her sunglasses onto the top of her head and smiled at them as they came closer. Her gaze grazed the scars on Cash's leg briefly before zipping back up and staying locked eye to eye.

"I'm Allegra." She thrust out her hand and stated the obvious, her raven black hair pulled into a high ponytail. "And this is Simon. Are you newlyweds? You look like you are. We got married here, so this place holds a special place in our hearts."

Her rapid-fire greeting surprised Isobel silent for a second. This was even more awkward than when people assumed she, Cash and Lottie were a family.

Before she could answer, Simon shook hands as well, his words picking right up where his wife left off. "There's definitely magic around here, since it was a small miracle our parents managed to stop bickering about our eco-friendly wedding theme long enough for us to say our vows. We got hitched in the ranch's big multi-wedding festival."

Isobel recalled some images of that in the promo material she'd reviewed for the ranch, everything from their eco-friendly event to a fairy-tale ceremony to another with a Scottish theme.

Allegra hooked arms with her husband. "Now we all get along fabulously. Love is definitely in the air in Moonlight Ridge." She winked before tipping her glasses back down to her nose. "Good luck."

The couple sprinted toward the dock, leaving all those assumptions behind them. Isobel rolled her eyes.

"Now, the two of them are loopy." When Cash didn't smile, she asked, "What are you thinking?"

"It's kind of a mood buster." He motioned forward. "Let's go ahead and check in with the tour guide."

She gripped his elbow, stopping him. "Tell me anyway."

Waiting, she felt like they were on the precipice of something, like a transition taking their friendship to a deeper level.

Friendship? Maybe more.

He exhaled in a gust and said, "I was wondering what your wedding to the jerk was like."

Oh. Wow. She wouldn't have guessed that in a million years, and it unsettled her. She searched for the words to answer him and could only come up with, "I never said he was a jerk."

"Your sister did," he confessed. "Based on what I've seen over the past months—or what I haven't seen—I believe Zelda. I know it's none of my business. I have no right."

Was her bad taste in a husband that obvious to everyone? Apparently so. A part of her protected his reputation for Lottie's sake. And, yes, another part of her was embarrassed to have believed his lies about forever devotion and fidelity.

"You're right." She crossed her arms tight over her chest even though the rising sun warmed her skin. "This is a mood buster. I found out I was pregnant with Lottie. Colin proposed. A friend of his had one of those online certificates to perform weddings."

"I'm sorry." Cash held up both hands in surrender. "That was none of my business."

"It's not a secret, and I shouldn't have insisted you tell me what you were thinking when you told me it would only dampen the day." She could feel all their intentions to have lighthearted fun slipping away. She reached to link fingers with him and lower his arms. "What do say we go whitewater rafting?"

His grip closed around her hand, and he drew her in for a quick hug. Her jaw went slack an instant before every nerve ending inside her came alive. His chin rested on the top of her head, his chest expanding with a deep breath before he stepped back.

A whistle sounded from the shore, drawing her attention away. Reluctantly.

Their whitewater rafting guide stood on a boulder. A guy around their age, there was a wild abandon about him, just the sort who thrived in this job and living on the edge. "Good morning, ladies and gentlemen. My name is Gil Hadley. I'm your guide for the next two hours. Are you ready for the ride of your lives?"

Cash's smile only gave her a moment's warning before he ducked his shoulder into her stomach and lifted her into a fireman's carry.

He palmed her bottom as he jogged toward the shore. "Don't start without us. Me and my girl are on our way."

She choked on a laugh, the tingling awareness mixing with joy into a heady champagne bubbling through her veins. He jogged down the slight hill toward the shore effortlessly.

A few feet away, she heard Allegra cheer. "What did I tell ya? Love is most definitely in the air."

Isobel grasped at the back of his shirt, staring down at the lush grass.

"Cash, you can put me down." Another giggle bubbled free. "You're going to hurt yourself."

His snort of disbelief rumbled against her before he eased her to the ground in a long, slow slide. She bit her bottom lip hard to stifle a moan.

One look at the yellow raft made her all too aware of how close she and Cash would be sitting together, body to body, for the next two hours. Today, she was most definitely living on the edge.

Two hours later, Cash was on the edge of losing his mind. And not just from the temptation of Isobel pressed against him with each jostle of the boat along waves or bump into a jutting boulder.

The joy on her face flipped his world even as they stayed secure in the raft. She took each jostle and rushing curve with enthusiasm. She sliced her paddle through the water, holding her own in steering and propelling them over the crashing waves.

He'd been worried she would regret the outing once they were underway, but she'd surprised him. He suspected she'd surprised herself as well.

How could he have missed this side of Isobel over the past months? He'd been so wrapped up in his own pain, he hadn't realized until now that he could have been a wet blanket on their time together back then.

How his behavior may have kept her from showing this side of herself.

Now, as the raft settled into a cruising speed paddling the last leg of their journey, he told himself it was for the best this outing was drawing to a close. Especially since he was struggling to keep his hands off her. He needed to escort her back to the cabin. Pronto. Then go for a very long run, followed by a cold shower.

Thankfully, soon the boat bumped against the dock, this one close to the famous Sulis Springs Cave. Their guide quickly secured both ends with a rope. Cash vaulted to the dock, reaching a hand down to help Isobel out. Surefooted, she launched up and into his arms. Thank goodness for the life jackets between them.

Her head tipped back, droplets glistening on her eyelashes. "That was incredible."

She spun away and hopped to shore, unbuckling her yellow helmet. One fastener at a time, she loosened her bright orange life vest, then gathered her ponytail into her hands and squeezed out the excess water.

Heaven help him.

Was the crisp mountain air here a little thin? Because he was feeling decidedly lightheaded. Everyone else seemed to be managing just fine as they stowed gear. Allegra and Simon waded in to recline on a boulder while their guide inventoried supplies.

He angled a quick glance at her before stacking his gear in the waiting cart. "I didn't know you were so adventurous."

"So, you expected me to freak out half way through

the journey." She tossed her jacket and helmet on top of his.

"I did think that, but you proved me wrong," he said, surprised he could string words together with her standing a foot away, looking sleek and enticing in her black swimsuit. The cutout notches up her sides almost drove him to his knees. "I seem to recall you demanded to be in the front of the boat, waves splashing in your face."

He wanted to pull her into his arms and see if she tasted as delicious as she looked. But even though he'd joked about being friends with benefits, he knew she deserved more—everything.

So he just had to keep his hands to himself and get them both back to the cabin.

She reached into her waterproof bag and pulled out her cell phone, scrolling quickly. "Looks like Lottie's having the time of her life." Isobel held up the screen to show him a photo of her daughter riding a pony, being led by the rodeo dude around barrels. "Neve is picking her up for lunch shortly. Lottie has been looking forward to cooking grilled cheese sandwiches over the campfire."

"I can't wait to hear all about it when we see her later," he said, making a mental note to take her next time. "Your sisters seem to be enjoying the time with Lottie."

"Accepting their help isn't easy," she said, some of the light dimming in her eyes, "especially when there's not much I can do in return."

"You do so much for others." He couldn't count the times she'd shown up at the PT facility with cookies for the staff or free books to share with other parents.

If someone expressed a preference, he could all but see Isobel planning to make it happen.

What would it have been like to meet her before his world fell apart in that fire? Before the regrets haunted him even in his sleep?

He would never know. "I guess we should start heading back now."

She planted her feet, that mischievous gleam filling her eyes again until the joy sparkled like the droplets on her lashes. "It's not even noon yet. Let's test out the hot springs."

How could he resist the request after he'd worked hard to encourage her to make time for herself? Even as he realized he might well regret it, he clasped her hand and followed her along the path into the dimly lit cavern.

Chapter Eleven

Isobel stepped into the steamy warmth of the Sulis Cave, the mild scent of sulfur tingeing the air with medicinal healing. She'd wanted to explore this aspect of the ranch, and now seemed like the perfect time, while her adrenaline was still high from the whitewater rafting excursion.

From sharing it with Cash.

His footsteps echoed softly as he followed her through the arched opening, along the path leading around a corner to a cavern with bubbling waters in the center. The space sprawled before her lit by dim lights recessed in stone. As Cash drew up beside her, the glow was low enough that his scars were almost indistinguishable. She squeezed his hand, wondering who had been there to comfort him immediately after the accident. He'd told her once that his girlfriend had bailed.

Unimaginable. And so sad Isobel pushed aside the thought for now before it tarnished the moment, like thoughts of her ex. No doubt, she and Cash were seeking to learn more about each other.

Ledges around the pool were large enough for benches and even a couple of two-person tables. In the far corner, there was a changing area, blocked off with cedar partitions. Another corner sported a pile of Bohemian pillows.

Even though they weren't alone, there was a sense of isolation, a timelessness, with the rest of the world sealed outside. The stone walls were covered with paintings: some sophisticated, others more childlike. Above them, red script spelled out *Art Therapy—Sharing Our Stories*. Hand-thrown pottery lined the walls beneath, images etched in some Grecian style.

Along with two other couples she didn't recognize, Simon and Allegra lazed, half submerged and sipping champagne as the steam rose around them. Allegra waved enthusiastically. "Welcome. There's more champagne and flutes on the table if you'd like."

Cash rested a warm hand on Isobel's shoulder. "I'm okay, but thanks." He angled a look at her. "Would you like me to pour one for you?"

Isobel shook her head, her mind already fizzing from his nearness. "No, thank you. Maybe later. For now, I just want to enjoy nature's hot tub."

She took Cash's hand and led him down the stone steps, pleasantly warm water lapping around her ankles, then thighs, until she launched into the center, her toes just touching the bottom.

Their whitewater rafting guide, Gil Hadley, reclined along the far edge of the pool on the opposite side of where the other couples congregated. "Best way to spend a lunch break. One of the many perks to the job."

Cash held Isobel's hand until she settled into one of the notched seats cut into the stone. When Gil didn't show signs of moving, she asked, "What brought you to the Top Dog Dude Ranch?"

"I grew up in Moonlight Ridge," Gil said, swiping a hand towel over his face, his black hair slicked back, "as did my father and my father's father."

She stifled a gasp, barely daring to hope someone in his family might be a source of information about Gran. "That's quite a legacy. My grandmother grew up here as well. Before she married, her name was Alice Franklin. Maybe someone in your family remembers her."

Gil scratched along his jaw. "Could be."

Isobel searched for the right words, aware of Cash's curious gaze. It didn't seem wise to lead with being in search of a kidney donor. "She passed away recently, and I've been trying to find out more about her early years. Honestly, when she spoke of the Smoky Mountains, I thought it was more of an embellished fairy tale. It all sounded too magical."

"Moonlight Ridge has to be experienced to be believed." Gil hitched an elbow along the ledge, his Top Dog T-shirt soggy. "You two were all in on the rafting ride today. A photo would have made the perfect advertisement."

Cash slid an arm around her shoulders. "Would you believe this was Isobel's maiden voyage?"

Gil whistled appreciatively. "Well, Isobel, you're a natural. I bet you have Sulis water running through your veins, compliments of your grandmother." He sat up straighter, then stood and grabbed his towel. "I'm going to leave you two to your soak and go take a quick swim before heading back to work for the afternoon shift."

Isobel called out, "Nice talking to you."

She'd hoped for more information, but at least she knew where to find him later.

Cash drew her closer, tucking her into a half hug. "That was promising."

The warmth and strength of his chest stirred a heat in her far more than the steaming waters. She hauled her focus back on his words. "I wish I could have asked if his father and grandfather are still alive, but I didn't want to freak him out with the third degree."

"I agree. We can look up his family easily enough on the internet." Frowning, he paused. "Would you like to leave and start that now?"

She appreciated that he'd offered her that out. She even considered it for a moment, then opted to stay put. "Let's stay just a little longer. It's not like it was a specific tip."

And she didn't want to shortchange Cash of the time to soak in these waters. Whether they held healing powers or not, the springs had to offer some therapeutic benefits for him.

Nodding, he trailed his fingers along her upper arm. "This space is incredible. The art on the wall, the pottery."

"The ranch certainly immerses its guests in their five senses, sparking creativity." As she sunk lower into the bubbling waters and leaned her head back on the ledge, her gaze scanned over the art. "I can imagine the stories in each one of those."

A child swimming with friends in a pond, celebrating.

A man sitting under a tree with his head in his hands. Mourning something?

A couple saddling up horses in what should have been a mellow, pastoral image. But the colors were darker, the edges of the images hazy. They each looked in a different direction, as if avoiding.

Cash continued to draw those simple but enticing circles along her arm. "What would you have painted?"

Her heart fluttered in her chest at his thoughtful attention. One of the things that had drawn her to him had been the way he really saw her. Not just as Lottie's mom and a fixture at the therapy center. But her—Isobel. It had been so long since she'd focused on herself, she'd almost forgotten how.

Now, she let her imagination spin for a moment before answering, "I would add Lottie and Cocoa to the story."

"Ah, with her wheelchair to show diversity."

"Actually, I would paint her walking, maybe even flying." Something that she could only do for her child through art. Her spine couldn't be repaired.

He scratched his chest right over his heart, staying silent.

She drew in a shaky breath, the steam filling her to the base of her soul. "I'm terrified. Every single day. Scared to death that something bad is going to happen to my daughter."

His light caresses turned to a comforting squeeze. "I can't even begin to imagine."

She appreciated that he didn't offer platitudes, and

that opened the floodgates. "When I got pregnant, I just assumed everything would be straightforward and easy. When the alpha-fetoprotein test came back high, even then I assumed the due date was off or that we were having twins. It just didn't cross my radar that there would be a problem."

The fear of that time steamrolled her all over again, her mind filling with the memory of sitting in her obstetrician's office. To this day, she could still feel the itchy fabric of the chair as she'd gripped the edge. "The ultrasound confirmed that our baby girl had a neural tube birth defect. She would need surgery within seventy-two hours of delivery. I have looked back a million times, analyzing everything I did, every bite I ate, trying to find what I did wrong that caused my child this struggle in life."

"Isobel, I don't know much of anything about pregnancy nutrition, but I've seen the great lengths you go to in educating yourself about every aspect of Lottie's care."

"Thank you," she said with a shaky smile, resting her head on his damp shoulder. "And now as if Lottie didn't already have enough to deal with, there's a kidney transplant. She six. Just six years old. It's not fair."

"You're right." He rested his chin on her head, his voice ragged. "It's horribly unfair. I'm not even her parent, and it's tearing my heart out thinking about her having that surgery. I would give anything at all if I could have been a match for her."

Shifting, she knelt in her stone seat. She took his face in her hands, his unshaven jaw bristly against her palms. "You helped me get here to Moonlight Ridge and search. You've gone above and beyond in helping my child. I'll never forget it."

He clasped her wrists but didn't move her touch away. "I don't need thanks or gratitude."

His eyes were full of compassion, of caring. He was such a good man. How could she not be drawn to him?

She slid her hands down to his chest. "Do you think we would have noticed each other and become friends if we'd crossed paths in some ordinary way, in line at the grocery store or on opposite sides of a gas pump?"

He folded his hand over hers and gripped it as firmly as his gaze held hers. "I most definitely would have noticed you anywhere, anytime."

The steam between them thickened, the air full of need and promise. Without hesitation, she let herself be drawn in, just for now in this timeless place full of fairy tales. "What would we have talked about in that hypothetical meet in the grocery store?"

He lifted her hand and pressed a kiss to her fingers. "I'd have asked you for help in understanding all the different kinds of lettuce."

The feel of his mouth lingered on her skin, launching a fresh rush of the fizzy champagne sensation through her veins.

"Smooth. Better than 'What's your sign?'"

His laugh tangled with hers, low and intimate in the sliver of space between them. The tingle of desire burned hotter, making her ache to explore the connection between them.

He swayed toward her, his mouth meeting hers for

a simple brush. One she held and returned. Nothing elaborate, given they were not alone, but so very moving for the emotion flowing between them, a friendship and respect deeper than any she'd felt before.

As they angled apart again and she saw the answering awareness in his eyes, she knew that time was running out to hold strong against their undeniable attraction. "Your girlfriend was a fool to let you go."

His forehead fell to rest against hers. "Thanks, but I wasn't much of a prize after the wreck."

She disagreed but could see his face closing, so she clasped his hands and drew him deeper into the center of the hot springs. No doubt, they both needed more than a little bit of healing.

Cash struggled to haul himself out of the grips of his nightmare. Yet the harder he thrashed in his bed, the heavier the weight of sleep anchored him in the horror. Part of his mind shouted at him to wake up, to leave the replay of his past blending with the present in a tormenting stew.

The cave yawned in front of him, dark and muted. Painted images on the wall began to move, coming to life. His friend Elijah suited up, riding on the truck. A scenario he'd lived out many times. Except Cocoa sat beside Elijah, and the fire engine drove past Isobel and Lottie. None of which made sense. They'd never met.

And while Cash held a megaphone in his hand, he couldn't bring it to his mouth. He needed to shout a warning to them all, make himself heard over the deafening siren. His throat closed up. His legs felt like they were made of lead, but he pushed through, walking, running beside the hook and ladder. He needed to be there with Elijah. But he also needed to keep Isobel and Lottie from seeing the world explode, from seeing how he had failed to save Elijah.

He struggled for an answer, but the steam swirling in the cave fogged his mind as well as his vision. Much longer and he would lose sight of them all, every one of them.

Desperate, he waved them toward the bubbling hot springs. If somehow he could sweep them all into the water, they would be safe. Healed. Alive.

The mist parted, giving him a glimpse of the fire truck, except now Cocoa wasn't sitting beside Elijah. Isobel sat in the spot normally occupied by Cash. And the truck began steering toward the pooling water.

Relief poured through him. The weights falling from his legs allowed him to run toward them, to join them, safe.

He launched, diving through the steam toward the swirling waters. Just as he went airborne, the mist became smoke…

Isobel threw aside her covers, craning to listen to the rustle that disrupted her sleep. Was it a branch brushing against the cabin? Or someone walking down the hall? She scrubbed a hand across her face to will away the fog of slumber and the urge to crawl back under the covers. It was only three in the morning after all.

Footsteps thudded slowly, softly, one after the other

past her door and toward the living area. Not a branch at all. Cash must be awake.

Even knowing it might not be wise after their steamy kiss earlier in the day, she slid her feet to the floor, the braided rug soft under her bare feet. She smoothed her long T-shirt and padded out into the dark hall. A light streamed from the kitchen and she kept walking, drawn to the glow. And, yes, drawn to the man.

Their swim had been playful and fun, both of them choosing to ignore that impulsive kiss. Then the rest of the day became a whirlwind of activity with Lottie returning from her horseback riding and cookout, eager to attend the game night at the dining hall for supper. The rest of the day and evening had been packed, then dinner, then Isobel had tucked her daughter in for the night. Cash had left for a late-night jog while she searched the internet for contact information about Gil's family. When Cash still hadn't returned, she decided she might as well turn in.

Was he avoiding her? Or had she been dodging him, hiding behind the busyness of motherhood and Lottie's PT appointments at the facility in Moonlight Ridge? Drawing in a bracing breath, she urged her feet the rest of the way into the kitchen.

Cash was searching through the refrigerator, setting the makings for a sandwich on the counter beside a loaf of bread—lunchmeat, cheese, mayonnaise. Plus three kinds of pickles. She'd learned that about him during their time here, and so much more.

How quiet the cabin would be when he left in a

week. How quiet her *life* would be. "Having trouble sleeping?"

He glanced back at her, the fire department T-shirt showcasing his broad shoulders. "A bit. And you?"

"I heard you and wanted to make sure Lottie hadn't woken you with an issue." A fib. Isobel kept her cell phone monitor on in case her daughter needed her. But she figured she would be forgiven for the little fib.

He nudged the refrigerator closed. "Sorry to wake you. Do you want a sandwich too?"

"Sure. I'll make mine though," she said, falling into a rhythm making their snack, a dance of sorts as they took turns piling on the deli slices. She thought about making light conversation. Certainly she would have done so in the past.

But they'd gone beyond that since arriving in Moonlight Ridge. Things would never be simple again. So she waited for him to share whatever was on his mind.

And if his heavy mood stemmed from regret over their kiss? A need to take a step away? She would handle it. She was a pro at bouncing back after life kicked her in the gut.

He passed her a bottle of sparkling water before taking one for himself, staying at the counter to eat. Two bites into his sandwich, he nudged his plate aside and braced both hands on the granite. "I have, uh, bad dreams. I guess you could call them night terrors, the PTSD kind."

Her chest squeezed tight at the knowledge that he dealt with that. He'd already been through so much. She held herself very still rather than risk startling him away. Instead, she kept her voice soft and low. "About the accident?"

Still he didn't face her, staying in profile, head low, jaw flexing. "I shouldn't have been at work that day."

She let the silence hang between them, waiting to see if he would say more, not wanting to interrupt him. When he stayed quiet for five heartbeats, she prodded carefully. "Did you get called in?"

He shook his head. "I was exhausted. I'd stayed out late helping my neighbor—my best friend—move. I wasn't just short on sleep, I'd worked my body hard lifting furniture. I should have taken a personal day."

Regrets and second guesses were a beast. She knew that all too well from looking back year after year in an attempt to make sense of her child's birth defect. "I'll say to you the same sort of thing you told me this afternoon. It sounds to me like you're being hard on yourself. It's tough to imagine that no firefighter, cop or doctor ever clocked in tired. That's life."

His throat moved in a long swallow. "It's just not that simple."

"Did you break a rule as far as what's mapped out by the station?" She knew he hadn't, that he wouldn't, and she hoped her question would make him see that.

"No, of course not. And I wouldn't still have a job if I had," he said, not looking in the least comforted.

"I'll say it again. You're judging yourself too harshly."

"How can I not?" His voice grew ragged as he slumped back against the counter. "My best friend— Elijah—died in the fire."

Wait. His friend? She'd assumed it was someone—a

civilian—trapped in the blaze. "The person you helped to move was the same man who died?"

He nodded.

Forget distance. She rested her hand on his back, her palm moving in circles as she searched for the right words to help him. "So your friend was just as tired and exhausted as you, maybe more so."

Cash cut his eyes toward her, a wildness in his gaze that startled her. "Isobel, I'm not going to blame him for what happened. Don't even go that route."

"I'm sorry," she said quickly, wishing she knew how to offer better comfort. "I didn't mean to upset you or disrespect his memory."

The anger faded from him as quickly as it had come, revealing deep pain. Then he closed his eyes and hauled her against his chest. "And I apologize for snapping."

Without hesitation, she wrapped her arms around him and hugged him close, anchoring herself as much as him. She breathed in the scent of detergent in his shirt, mingling with a hint of perspiration. A manly blend uniquely Cash.

She rested her head against his steady heartbeat. "Perhaps it's time we both cut ourselves some slack for being human beings who are trying the very best we can."

His "hmmm" vibrated against her ear as they stood, taking their time in the embrace. The clock ticked through minutes as neither of them moved. Deeper and deeper she sunk into the sensation of him—of them together. The rightness and warmth of it enveloped her in much the same way as the hot springs waters had closed around her earlier in the day. More than anything, right now, she wanted to dive right in. Consequences could be faced later.

Then his head moved, just a hint as he nuzzled along her jawbone. All the encouragement she needed. Desire shot through her, stirring all the awareness she'd stuffed down these last weeks. Isobel turned into his kiss, fully pressing her body closer to his. Aching to be nearer still.

She tunneled her hands up under that washed soft T-shirt of his, exploring the hard muscled planes of his chest. A hoarse moan rumbled from him into her, and his hands roved up her back and into her hair. It had been so long since she'd felt a man's touch. And even her memory couldn't draw up a moment as incredible as this.

The truth unfurled inside her. She wanted him. All of him. Tonight. Even knowing he would leave. She refused to live with the regret of never having made love with Cash. Now all she needed was a sign from him that he longed for the same.

As their kiss ended, her lashes fluttered open and she looked into his eyes filled with desire.

"Isobel," he groaned.

"Cash," she answered, slipping her hand in his and leading him to her bedroom.

Chapter Twelve

Cash knew he was in serious trouble.

As he reclined in Isobel's bed hours later, head deep in the down pillow, he couldn't remember when he'd been so moved by a woman. Making love with Isobel had stirred something inside him, something more than the physical.

Could it simply be their friendship connection? Certainly all his past relationships had started with romance, then moved to sex. Some became friends later as well. But no experience came close to what he'd felt tonight.

Maybe the nightmare had his feelings raw and exposed, until all sensation brushed against his tender soul. That would be an easy answer, one that didn't require further analysis.

But simple was rarely right.

He kept his silence, watching her rise from the bed in the dim light as early morning rays slanted through the wooden shutters covering the window. Isobel pulled a T-shirt over her head, a Cocoa the Canine logo across the front. She reached into the closet, the stretch revealing her teal-colored panties. His body stirred, and he ached to peel her clothes back off her again as he'd done a few hours ago.

Except he knew they were running out of time fast in so many ways. First and foremost, Lottie would be waking soon, which meant he needed to hightail it back to his own room. Soon. After he indulged himself in watching Isobel dress.

She pulled folded jeans from the shelf and tugged them on one leg at a time. With every inch she covered, his mind reversed the action to reveal the memory of discovering her body for the first time.

As if she felt the weight of his gaze, Isobel looked back at him quickly. "Oh, I didn't mean to wake you. I'm sorry."

He scooted up to lean against the brass headboard, rustling the sheets and releasing the scent of her from the red checkered bedspread. Sleep wasn't in the cards for him. It never was after a nightmare. "There's no need for you to sneak off."

"I wasn't running away," she assured him, although she avoided his eyes, making a big ordeal out of finding a pair of socks. "I'm just going to rustle up some breakfast. In case you hadn't noticed, even if I was hotfooting it out of the room, we're staying in the same cabin. It won't be difficult to locate me."

True enough. Still something in her demeanor gave off a restlessness he couldn't name. "That we are."

"For another week."

Ah. Was she upset over him going? Or wondering what this meant regarding how they would spend the remainder of his time here together? "Is that a proposition to make the most of that time?"

The answer wasn't apparent on her face.

She sat on the bed again, tugging on the socks then crisscrossing her legs. "I'm not sure. This was incredible," she waved over the rumpled bedspread, "so much so my mind hasn't reengaged enough for me to think through the implications."

Implications? That sounded ominous. "Fair enough."

"But we will talk," she promised. "Later."

All right. He could live with that. In fact, he preferred her wait-and-see approach.

He stroked a hand down her leg. "Incredible, huh?"

"You know it was." A smile spread across her face, the unease disappearing to reveal the Isobel he knew so well. She angled down to give him a kiss, lingering as her hand fell to his bare chest. "I'll see you at breakfast?"

"I wouldn't be anywhere else," he assured her, perhaps himself as well.

After another quick kiss, she scooted off the bed and out into the hall, leaving him more confused than ever. How was there such a sense of uncertainty between them mixed with this heightened awareness? Yet, he wouldn't take away what they'd just shared for anything.

He just had to figure out how to be around her. Fast. Because their time together was coming to an end, and he refused to dishonor their friendship by leaving on a negative note.

Yes, she was avoiding Cash.

Isobel admitted it to herself, but the notion sounded awful to say out loud. She needed time to sift through the shift in their relationship before they talked about what happened next. Would she be able to indulge in a one week fling with a friend who would be leaving soon? Could she hold her emotions in check, knowing this move could quite possibly be the last time she saw him?

She also couldn't envision asking for any kind of commitment after how badly her marriage had imploded. Not even a long-distance romance.

But, wow, last night had rocked her to the core. Cash had been passionate and tender, her friend and her lover all at once wrapped up in a muscular body that made her ache to dive right in for more.

"Are you listening?" Zelda tapped her on the head.

Isobel blinked the fog from her mind until she was once again mentally present with her sisters on the cabin's front porch. They'd opted for lunch together here, away from the world, to give them a chance to visit uninterrupted. Plus, Lottie was resting inside with Cocoa before the archery class late this afternoon.

Cash was long gone after eyeing her warily at breakfast. He'd left right afterward for a trail ride. It must be an extended one, because she still hadn't seen or heard from him. She tried not to let that sting. That would be hypocritical since she needed the time to consider her next move.

Now that she and her sisters had finished their sandwiches, Isobel thrust her hands through her hair, gathering it back and sweeping a hair scrunchie off her wrist. "I was just thinking about the next topic for my blog."

Only a tiny fib since, more than likely, somehow her post would revolve around an issue with Cash. Her writings always did lately.

Zelda stroked her Maltese in her lap, looking a bit like Dr. Evil from the Austin Powers movies as she eyed Isobel with skepticism. "You look like a woman who didn't get much sleep. Is there a reason for that you'd care to share?"

"Nope," Isobel said before lifting her Yeti for a sip of lemon water.

Neve laughed softly. "Message received. You prefer not to share. Moving along. What did you find out about this Gil Hadley guy?"

Grateful for the reprieve—both in their conversation and in her own thoughts—Isobel refocused on what mattered most to her right now. She had more work to do to find a Lottie a donor.

"He grew up here in Moonlight Ridge, as he said," Isobel rolled through the info she'd found online and from Hollie O'Brien, "then he went off to college, toured the world a bit, hiked some mountains. Seems like a real adventurous type. Then he returned home about a year ago."

Neve tapped her rocking chair into motion, tipping her face toward the overhead fan. "And what about the rest of his family?"

"His father and grandfather are from Moonlight Ridge as well," Isobel said, feeling a bit like a snoop for all the digging she'd done online. "The grandfather passed away a few months ago. He was a few years ahead of Gran in school, so they wouldn't have crossed paths."

Zelda frowned. "That's disappointing. It seems like we keep hitting brick walls."

Neve kept a steady pace with her rocker, as even as a metronome. "It's early yet. Reliable research takes time and patience."

True, but that didn't help the frustration. The worry. Isobel waited for a family with fishing poles to pass in front of the cabin. For once little Sebastian wasn't chasing after his teenage sisters. She stuffed down a twinge of envy for that family.

Once they passed, Isobel continued. "Gil's dad still lives here. It's a long shot, but I've reached out to him via email and will follow up with a call."

Zelda set her senior pup on the ground and little Maisey trotted out into the fenced yard, pausing to sniff pansies in the dog-safe garden. "I met one of the older stable hands who's from the area. He hadn't heard of Gran, but he gave me some names to look up. I'll text them to you."

Zelda pulled out her phone and tapped out a quick message. Isobel scooped up her cell to confirm the text came through, finding that she'd also missed three calls from her ex. She hoped it hadn't been anything urgent. But there weren't any messages explaining what he'd wanted.

Neve spread her hands, her nails short and neat. "Sorry to say, I've come up empty, but I'm not giving up. I'm in this for the long haul."

Setting her phone aside, Isobel squeezed her elbow. "No need to apologize. I know you've given it your best, as you do everything in life."

Neve managed a half smile. "I may come off like Mary Sunshine sometimes, but I do understand the gravity of what we're trying to achieve for Lottie. It's not just about Gran's final wish."

"Thank you," Isobel said, looking from one sister to the other, thankful to have their support, "I can't express how much it means to me to have you both here."

Both sisters reached for one of her hands. The connection defied any time spent apart. They shared a history, a bond, an understanding on a deep-rooted level beyond any simple squabbles. The connection felt stronger than ever after losing their parents and Gran.

Neve squeezed harder before letting go, her eyes sympathetic and so like Gran's right now. "How do you feel about Cash leaving?"

Isobel should have known she couldn't dodge their curiosity—concern really—much longer. She settled for a truthful answer, even if it was only part of the equation. "He's starting at a new fire station. Returning to his old life. That's a good thing."

"Ahem." Neve leveled a take-no-bull look at her, even more so like Gran. "That's not what I was really asking."

Isobel scratched her fingernail along the back of her phone case, sighing at her sister's perceptiveness. "I would be sad about any friend moving."

Rolling her eyes, Zelda snorted on a wry laugh. "You two don't look at each other like buddies."

Isobel sunk deeper into her rocker, the sensations and memory of last night rolling over her again in delicious detail. "I guess you would call us friends with benefits."

"Really?" Zelda squeaked. "You've been keeping that under your hat all this time?"

"Not *all* this time," Isobel hedged.

"How long then?" Neve asked dryly. "Not that it's any of my business, but I'm gonna ask anyway."

"Since last night," Isobel blurted. So much for keeping the information to herself.

"Whoa." Zelda whistled softly before leaning forward to whisper, "How was it?"

She searched for the right way to describe the seamless joining of their bodies, the instinctive understanding they'd shared in knowing just what the other wanted. A wordless communication. Heat burned along her cheeks, and she settled for saying, "It was the best."

"The best? As in *the* best ever?" Zelda squealed again, leaning back in her rocker and kicking her feet. Even Neve offered up a little cheer.

But Isobel was frozen by the realization spreading through her. She couldn't muster a sound since her throat was closing up like she was trapped on the curviest of mountain roads with no shoulder between her and the sheer drop off.

If last night's encounter with Cash was her best sex ever, what if there was never again a time—a person—to match this moment? And that left her with a deep sadness, an empty hollow in her chest that defied explanation.

Fresh from his lengthy trail ride, Cash tucked into the spectator cluster like the other parents watching the archery class. He wasn't a parent. Still, he wouldn't have missed Lottie's big Robin Hood debut for anything.

In the clearing, six circular targets were perched on easels. The children waited behind the line to shoot their miniature crossbows. Thick ropes encircled the space to keep observers well clear of any possible stray misfires.

He scanned the rest of the crowd gathered on the other side until his gaze landed on Isobel with her sisters. The sun streamed down on her loose dark hair. His hands clenched around the memory of those silky strands sliding through his fingers. He'd been battling back those kinds of memories all day long, their time together thoroughly imprinted on his mind.

Clearing his throat, he shifted his attention to the kids, searching for Lottie. There were quite a few children gathered waiting their turn, some guests and others the offspring of staff members—the O'Brien twins, the librarian's son and, if he wasn't mistaken, the doctor's two grandchildren. And, of course, little Sebastian.

Finally, he located Lottie, and before he could second-guess the impulse, he shouted, "Go get 'em, Lottie."

At the sound of his voice, she looked over at him, waving, her smile bright as she sat so proudly in her jeans, plaid shirt and fringed vest. She wore a shiny sheriff's badge that he'd given her earlier in the week. As she rolled up to take her turn, he gave her a thumbs-up just before she raised her bow, taking careful aim…

The arrow flew.

He held his breath, all but willing the missile to

stay true in its path. He wanted her to feel the rush of success. Which was silly. His love for this kid wasn't dependent on what she did or didn't do. But he would move heaven and earth for her to get her heart's desire.

Bull's-eye.

Cash whooped, punching the air with his fist. Even if all the rest of her shots went haywire, she was the first kid to hit the target dead in the center. They would have to celebrate later.

And in that moment of pride, his gaze collided with Isobel's, the two of them linked in their joy for Lottie's success, whether they were standing together or not.

He felt petty for taking up a post to watch so far away from her. But he didn't know how to explain his need to give her the space she seemed to require. Their breakfast had been friendly but…off somehow. He didn't want her to feel pressured by what happened or weighted down by any sense of expectation from him. Besides, he needed to get his head together too. He didn't want to speak further while he was still flailing inside over what their encounter meant going forward.

A hand clapped him on the shoulder, hauling his attention back to the present. He looked back fast to find…the ranch's owner.

"Hello there, Jacob," Cash said, hands in his jeans pockets. "I see two of your children over there about to compete."

"Phillip and Elliot have been looking forward to this all week." He beamed with pride at his younger two boys. "I see your girl Lottie took the prize in her age group."

Cash didn't bother correcting him. Given his pride moments ago, it would have been rather hypocritical to deny the affection he felt for the child. "I'm sure she'll be framing the ribbon."

"We're going to be sad to see you leave next week," Jacob said with obvious sincerity. "It's been nice getting to know you."

Cash shook his head. "I bet you say that to all the guests."

"Actually, no," Jacob confessed. "Some can be a real pain in the butt."

"I can only imagine," Cash said. "I've had some humdinger experiences in my years as a firefighter. We got a call from a gentleman reporting a fire in his home. Except, turns out he wasn't there. He'd somehow figured out his wife had another man in their bedroom and thought having firefighters pound on the door would be embarrassing karmic justice."

Jacob laughed softly. "My stories aren't so funny. Like this couple attending a big family reunion. They were planning to file for divorce once the trip was over. They worked so hard not to argue, they ended up taking out all their frustration on the staff."

Cash winced. "I imagine it would be tough to keep your cool."

"Sometimes," Jacob said, "but I wouldn't trade this job for any other. Oh look, here comes Elliot to fire his arrow."

Cash turned to watch the boy lift his crossbow, understanding Jacob's pride in seeing his stepson's accomplishments. They both whistled for him when he hit the outer ring of the bull's-eye.

When the applause died down and the next child stepped up to fire an arrow, Cash recalled what Jacob said about loving his work here at Top Dog. He understood that love of a job, so much more than a career but being able to live out your dream. And right there was the crux of his dilemma. Knowing what he was meant to do but fearing he would fail again.

Having met Isobel during this time in his life made everything—work, the way he felt about her—all the more complicated. "I, for one, am glad you're the man in charge here. It's been a one-of-a-kind vacation."

"Thanks," Jacob said. "We still have the summer festival before you leave. You'll get to see all the ranch has to offer in full force."

"I look forward to it." Yet, even as he said the words, he couldn't ignore that the event also signaled the end of his time with Isobel. And, yes, Lottie too.

Jacob rocked back on his bootheels. "How's the search for relatives in the area going?"

"We've gotten names to look into," Cash said, welcoming the change of subject. Even as frustrating as the mission might be, at least it offered a tangible task to attack. To complete. "We've searched library records until our eyes are bleeding. But there are some holes in the data because of a courthouse fire a couple of decades ago."

"That's right." Jacob snapped his fingers. "I hadn't thought about that in a while. Citizens all up and down

Main Street risked their lives hauling as much out as possible before the whole place went up in flames."

Cash scratched the back of his neck, his scar heating with a phantom pain from the accident. From the dreams that haunted him still. "I hope no one was injured."

"No fatalities. A little smoke inhalation. A small miracle it wasn't worse," Jacob added somberly. "Well, for what it's worth, we're going to look after Isobel and Lottie when you leave. They've become honorary members of the Top Dog Dude Ranch family."

And whether Jacob intended the implication or not, his words left behind the undeniable reality that in leaving, Cash wouldn't be a part of that "honorary family" any longer.

Chapter Thirteen

While rain pattered outside the window, Isobel bustled around the kitchen, putting away the dishes and wiping off the counter so all would be tidied before they left for the family Bingo event. She and Cash had been steering clear of each other for most of the day, awkward in some ways but likely less so than having to face the radical shift in their relationship.

Truth be told, though, she missed him—her friend. In some ways she wished he was leaving now, because seeing him and wanting him while waiting for him to go was torture. So she focused on the mundane to distract herself, like scrubbing the farmhouse sink for a third time.

Lottie sat at the kitchen table with her coloring pencils and a pad of paper. She'd been illustrating a book of her summer adventures at the Top Dog Dude Ranch— Aunt Neve's idea, ever the academic with stellar ideals for making learning fun. Isobel, Zelda and Neve had joined in periodically, adding a flower here or a horse there. It felt a bit like chiming in during Gran's stories until the tales were family affair.

Finished with the tree trunk, Lottie dropped three

different colors of brown back into the box. A big bull's-eye was nailed in place. Apparently, her daughter was taking poetic license with the details, ditching the target tripods in her retelling of the event.

"Mommy," Lottie called out, her eyes still trained on her task as she plucked out greens for the leaves, "is Cash coming with us to Family Bingo?"

Isobel's gaze skirted to the hall, to his bedroom door. Still closed, thank goodness. He'd come through to change after an afternoon of fishing was cut short by rain clouds, arriving back at the cabin just as the sky opened up. She shushed her daughter. "Sweetie, he may have other plans for his day. Remember, he's here as our friend."

"But he's more than that. He's your boyfriend. That's what everybody thinks." She chewed the end of her pencil.

Isobel perched a hand on her hip. "And who is 'everybody'?"

"My friends—Elliot, Phillip, Ivy," she counted off on her fingers, "the triplets too. And Benji told me his uncle kept saying he and the library lady were just friends. Then they got married. Gus told me the same thing happened with his grandpa and Mrs. Eliza—that's the lady who runs the stables. I love riding the horses."

Following the path of her thoughts tangled up with so many names proved a challenge. But Isobel focused on the main point. "It doesn't matter what other people think or what might have happened to them. It's not true in this case."

"Why not? You guys are just right for each other." Lottie seesawed her pencil just like Neve, tapping the tabletop rhythmically. "You need him and he needs us."

This conversation wasn't going to be resolved as easily as she'd hoped, but it needed to be settled quickly—before Cash came out of his room. If he hadn't overheard already.

Isobel scraped a chair back from the table and sat, plucking up a yellow pencil to sketch a sun in the corner of Lottie's drawing, rays beaming down on a puppy in the crowd. "Life doesn't work that way. We don't just pick people to like. You have to love each other."

"Well, I love Cash." Lottie switched to pink and started sketching hearts in the sky like big puffy clouds. "Don't you?"

The question sent a bolt of downright fear through Isobel. This was not a discussion she wanted to have with her daughter—with anyone. She settled for a simple explanation. "Boyfriend and girlfriend love is different from love for a buddy."

"How do you know?" Lottie asked, scribbling harder and her until the paper threatened to tear. Her jaw jutted with the stubborn tilt that broadcast loud and clear she wasn't giving up that easily. "You thought you loved Daddy, and you were wrong. Maybe you're wrong about *not* loving Cash."

"Sweetie," Isobel said, setting aside her yellow pencil and clasping her hands around her daughter's until Lottie stopped coloring. "I know you want him to be in our lives, but it can't happen, not the way you want."

"Why not?" Tears welled in her blue eyes, hovering on her lids.

Those two tiny drops broke Isobel's heart. She searched for the right words to explain to her daughter.

A door opening and closing in the hallway broke the silence. Lottie scrubbed her wrist under her eyes and blinked fast. Isobel drew in a shaky breath. Her daughter's smile was so fast and seemingly genuine it made Isobel wonder how many times she may have been fooled in the past. She covered her daughter's hand and gave her a gentle squeeze. They would talk later. But not in front of Cash.

As he walked into the great room, Cash scrubbed a hand through his damp hair. "What have you two been up to while I was out?"

Isobel pulled a tight smile she hoped was as convincing as her daughter's. "I've been writing and Lottie's been creating stories of her own as well."

"Cash, Cash, look at my picture of target shooting." She pointed. "That's a magic arrow. See the stars all around it?"

He leaned over the table to look, his wet hair clumped together in the back until Isobel could see the small burn scar on his neck. "Wow, that's really great. What will that magic missile do when it strikes the bull's-eye?"

Lottie trailed her fingers over her artwork, her eyes glittering like Gran's in the throes of storytelling. "The tree will turn into fairy cabin full of elves that grant magic wishes. Do you think that makes a good tale, Cash?"

"Excellent, Lottie," he said, studying the picture intently. "In fact, it's so realistic-looking, I'm tempted to make a list of my wishes for those mystical creatures."

Lottie giggled, her tears long gone. "That's silly."

"Do you mind if I add something to the picture like your mom did?" After she nodded, he pulled out a red pencil and quickly drew a fire hydrant. "What's on the agenda for the rest of the day now that the storm clouds are about to open up on us?"

Backing from the table, he side-stepped Cocoa's tail sticking out from under the table. As he strode toward the kitchen, he ruffled the child's hair on his way to the coffee pot.

Isobel said, "Nothing exciting."

At the same time, Lottie exclaimed, "Bingo!"

Isobel groaned inside. So much for keeping her distance. Already, she knew exactly how Cash would answer. Because he was a good man, kind and careful not to hurt her daughter's feelings. Which made the impending farewell all the tougher.

Cash pulled out a coffee much and reached for the glass carafe. "I love a good game of Bingo. Count me in."

Cash hadn't played Bingo since his third grade classroom Halloween party. Yet here he was, striding into one of the ranch's barns for game night, and he had no idea why he'd agreed.

From what he'd heard, the wide-open space was also used for large parties and receptions. A stage was set up at the far end with a table and massive round cage with the numbers. Other tables formed lines, each with two cards and an ink dauber. Caramel corn and lemonade were available—this place had food down to an art form.

As rain hammered the roof, he trailed Isobel and her sisters, Lottie leading the way with Cocoa. When the little girl had asked him to accompany them to Family Bingo, he'd mulled over ways to bow out—until he saw the panicked look on Isobel's face. The realization had sunk in that she didn't want him to come. Since he'd been considering turning in early and listening to the rain on the roof, he'd been surprised at his own answer.

He still didn't know why he'd insisted, but he was all in, taking a seat next to Lottie with Cocoa underneath, Simon and Allegra to his left. The cards were printed with images that reflected the ranch's focus—like horseshoes, lassos, Stetsons, saddles, sheriff's stars and, of course, pawprints.

A table with prizes filled one corner. Stuffed toy dogs and horses for kids. Gift baskets of baked goods. Jewelry made from crystals mined in the cave, crafted by a local artisan everyone called River Jack. Isobel and her sisters were inspecting the loot, their three heads close together.

Cash lined his cards up side by side. "Fair warning, I'm crazy lucky at Bingo."

Grinning, Lottie showed off the gap from the tooth she'd lost two days ago. "Maybe I am too."

Cash winked at her. "Then we'll rake in all the prizes."

Lottie's face scrunched. "I wouldn't want to get everything, 'cause that would make the other kids sad. I just want to win one of those pretty pieces of jewelry for my mommy."

His heart squeezed in his chest. "Did you know that you're the very best kid ever?"

Lottie tipped her head with a playful air. "Well, I should sure hope so."

With a burst of laughter, Cash enjoyed the release of tension, almost able to forget about the approaching departure date.

Lottie tapped her dauber all along the edges of her card, making a boarder of circles. "I like this Top Dog place—a lot."

"Me too," he agreed, meaning every word. The ranch had offered him a space to breathe, which he hadn't had in a long while. "It's a great vacation spot."

"Yeah, I know it's not home." She replaced the cap on her ink dauber with undue focus. "I have a daddy back in Montana."

Her words flew in out of left field, delivering a sucker punch. Followed by a quick wash of guilt. Lottie wasn't his child. He had no right to be jealous of the guy she called Dad, a guy Cash had yet to cross paths with in six months.

More importantly, what did she mean by the comment? Because the last thing he wanted was to disrupt her family. "I know you do, kiddo."

"He and Mommy aren't married like Elliot's parents. His mom and dad live in the same house, and they have the same bedroom," she said matter-of-factly.

"Uhm…" He scratched a hand along the back of his

neck as the rain increased outside. He didn't know what to say in response to that. It seemed like a random conversation for children to have. And not one he cared to discuss. "How about I get us some snacks. That caramel popcorn looks—"

"No, thank you." She tugged a red pencil from the bag looped to the arm of her chair and wrote her name at the top of each card. "I only know this stuff because some of the kids around here think you're my daddy because we stay in the same cabin."

That must have been how the conversation progressed to talk about where mommies and daddies sleep. Man, he wished Isobel was here to handle this increasingly uncomfortable chat. "Your mom and I are very good friends."

Even saying that felt inadequate to explain the connection between them. The attraction. Beyond that, the urge to spend time together doing simple things, like walks and fishing. Sharing a pimento cheese sandwich and a bottle of water. Things he'd dreamed of sharing with his ex-girlfriend, and yet now, he felt…like damaged goods.

Already he could hear Isobel's voice in his head telling him that was wrong. But it didn't matter. Even the sound of her sweet tones couldn't drown out the roar inside him that hadn't quieted since he woke up after the fire.

Thankfully, he was saved from having to scramble up a better answer as Hollie O'Brien stepped up onto the stage, taking the microphone. "Is anyone feeling lucky tonight?"

* * *

Isobel toyed with the crystal keychain Lottie had won—and promptly given to her. Had Cash prompted her? She still didn't understand why he'd insisted on tagging along.

Her gaze skated across the barn where he stood with Troy by the open barn door, rain still sheeting outside. Objectively speaking, both men were handsome in a tall, broad-shouldered kind of way. Like many other cowboys scattered throughout the gathering.

So, why was it she felt so drawn to Cash above all the rest?

Since the rainstorm continued, the O'Briens had set up more indoor activities after the Bingo tournament. Tables had been rearranged to create a dance floor in front of the dais. The town sheriff himself was taking on DJ duties—apparently having been roped in by his wife, the ranch's head landscaper. All the residents of Moonlight Ridge seemed connected in one way or another.

The dusty dance floor was full all the way to the DJ's dais, both adults and children dancing—including Lottie.

When the music started, dancers had rushed to join in, the hoedown sound bringing a lively vibe. Before Lottie even had a chance to feel sad or left out, the oldest O'Brien boy—Freddy—was already pushing her chair in step with the rest of them.

Isobel sagged back against a support post, taking in the sight of her daughter so happy and at ease. As one song blended into another, sometimes Lottie steered her chair herself, and others—like during the conga line—her new little buddy Sebastian navigated for her. It wasn't that Lottie was the star of the show. It was more that she was a part of the crowd. The children here welcomed her as their friend, they saw past the chair to Lottie, a bright and funny child.

A hand fell to rest on her shoulder, and she knew without looking Cash had joined her.

He drew up alongside her. "She's having fun. How much longer before she'll be ready to return to the cabin? I can get the umbrella."

She shook her head. "Lottie asked to join the rest for movie time starting in a few minutes. The kids are gathering in a back room of the barn so the adults could continue dancing." She stopped short, not wanting him to think she was hinting at anything. "I'm enjoying the music and the snacks. Great inspiration for a blog."

No doubt, tonight's "Boot Scootin' Boogie" had set the barn alive. The sound of heels shuffling along the planked floor created a percussion in time with the music. Denim and plaids filled the dim space, bodies moving en masse.

Wordlessly, he held out his hand, asking, inviting, without pressure. In this moment, her old friend was back, and without hesitation, she linked her fingers with his. She followed him, stepping into his arms as they tucked their bodies into a gap in the crowd.

Their feet moved in sync through two songs, neither of them speaking. For a big, bold man, he danced with athletic grace, his hard, muscled body moving in perfect time with the upbeat music. Then a slower country ballad drew them closer to one another.

Closer still as the lyrics of "Always on My Mind" filled the room.

Then his cheek rested on top of her head, and she melted against his chest. She breathed in the earthy scent of him, the evergreen scent of his soap mingling with a hint of perspiration. The heady mixture reminded her of their night together.

There was something comforting too about knowing this couldn't go any further. She had to stick around for Lottie, and he'd offered to walk them back with the umbrella.

So, for now, she could just enjoy the delicious pleasure of a night dancing with a handsome man. "Thank you for coming tonight. I wouldn't have thought you're a Bingo king."

"I owed her a celebration for her outstanding performance at archery this afternoon." Cash's hand palmed Isobel's back—warm, strong. "And to be fair, Lottie won more often than I did. I just helped her mark her card."

She tried hard not to compare him to Colin. It wasn't fair to either man. But she couldn't help thinking about the times Colin had been a no-show for big events— like Lottie's graduation from kindergarten. Seeing her child scan the crowd looking for her father...made Isobel hurt and furious all at once.

Her fingers clenched tighter around Cash's. "It meant a lot to her that you came to watch. It meant a lot to me too." She tipped her head back. "I know we've talked about you being free to pursue other events—ones that don't involve kids."

"I've gone trail riding, fishing—"

"Cash," she shushed him with a light touch to his mouth. "I'm asking why you keep coming with us—beyond what a good friend would do."

His face furrowed in thought, as if he didn't quite understand either. What a mess they'd made of their unexpected friendship.

Finally, he sighed, his eyes downcast. "I've wondered the same thing, and I can't come up with a clear-cut answer. Suffice it to say, this is the closest I've felt to family fun in a very long time."

A hint of unease skittered up her spine. Because she was afraid of his words? Or because she wanted… more? She searched for a benign way to nudge them off this detour in the conversation. "You've mentioned your dad being very involved."

His shoulders relaxed and he swayed closer, his boots shuffling. "Mom too, when she wasn't pulling extra shifts at the hospital." His eyes filled with nostalgia. "We used to bake together. We were all on such different schedules, it was rare for us to sit down for breakfast or dinner together. Mom said baking together gave us a connection when we all ate the muffins or the biscuits for meals."

"That's really lovely." She could envision him as a little boy with his own apron and flour on his hands. Maybe even a hint of batter on the corners of his mouth. "Where do your parents live now?"

His smile faded. "They're both gone."

"Oh no," she gasped softly. "I'm sorry for bringing up painful memories." Her own parents' death still hurt in a way she wasn't sure would ever fully resolve.

"It's okay," he said, resting his head on top of hers, his face shielded from view. "They passed away in a fluke car accident. A driver in the oncoming lane fell asleep at the wheel and drifted into their lane. Dad had gone to pick Mom up from a late shift because her car was in the shop."

"That's just terrible." She'd wondered about his solitary life before, but it had seemed rude to ask why no one ever drove him to and from rehab on the difficult days. The first time she'd seen him shuffle his crutches into an Uber, she'd been stunned. "How long ago did this happen?"

"Two years ago." His voice rumbled in his chest, against her ear. "I wasn't at the station that day. My buddy Elijah got called to the scene. He came to my apartment to give me the news personally."

She held her breath so she wouldn't gasp and risk making him feel even worse. She didn't even know what to say to that. So she just held him a little tighter while they swayed. Giving him the time he needed to sift through the emotions of what he'd just shared.

But thank heaven Cash hadn't been at work that day. She couldn't imagine how much more traumatic that would have been for him. Although, she also wondered if this connection between his parents and Elijah had made the death of his friend carry a double blow. Like a lost thread between Cash and his folks. Heartbreakingly tragic on so many levels.

Cash cleared his throat and continued, "I always thought of the word 'orphan' as applying to a child who'd lost both parents. I never considered how it would feel when referring to an adult. How had I never considered how my folks felt when their moms and dads passed away?"

She tucked her face into the crook of his neck. "We have that in common, the two of us. No parents. No grandparents left alive. It's strange to be the senior generation, especially this young."

"Maybe that's part of what drew us to befriend each other, a search for..."

"Family."

And there it was. The conversation had circled right back around to how it started. Except now she had said the same to him. Did it sting him the way it had her? Talking about family rather than the attraction. This dance was feeling increasingly like a goodbye.

His sigh rustled her hair. "You have your sisters now. I'm glad of that."

So now he could leave her? No worries or obligations. Maybe that was what this honorable man had been searching for in this trip. A way to close the door on their friendship without having to feel guilty over leaving.

And as much as that made her wince, she also couldn't stop wondering, who did he have? Her heart squeezed in her chest with sadness for him, a sense of helplessness swelling, because there was nothing she could do to fix this for him, definitely not long distance.

Even if she wanted to, following him wasn't an option because of Lottie. And never again would she haul herself all around the country for a man.

A resurgence of anger at Colin washed over her, stronger than she'd felt in a very long time. He'd been offered three different positions, one of which was closer to her family. But he'd insisted on taking the Montana-based job. He'd insisted it would be an adventure, that *he* was her nuclear family.

Now she wondered if he'd just wanted to isolate her from her family, from people who might have lent a sympathetic ear to her suspicions. Or simply, having family close would have given her a place to leave.

Had she ignored the signs of his cheating out of fear of being alone to bring up their child?

That notion felt more than a little uncomfortable. It had been easier to blame Colin for the whole mess— and no doubt, he was the one who'd broken his vows.

One thing shone through the tangled mess of emotions. She had her family back, her sisters, and she wasn't giving them up again.

And if this was goodbye between her and Cash? She'd survived plenty of heartbreak in her life. She would get past this.

She had no choice.

Chapter Fourteen

Cocoa the Caring Canine

Dancing is a funny thing. Humans swing and cuddle all around the dance floor. But if my feet are set into motion like that, I'm told to settle down.

Luckily, my person gives me all sorts of playtime to get my wriggles out. Running around the fenced yard. Playing fetch with my girl. The very best bones and a Kong filled with frozen peanut butter. (That's my favorite.)

If we don't find ways to vent our pent-up feelings, they explode in a wriggle fit. Or even worse...

The creak of the gate opening drew Isobel's attention from the computer screen as she worked from the porch in the midafternoon warmth.

Her sister Zelda waved, holding two wine glasses and a bottle. "Care to take a work break?"

"I would love to." Isobel closed her laptop and tucked it underneath her oak rocker. She loved being able to write outside, soaking up the sounds and smells of nature while Lottie napped a simple door away. "I've more than written my quota for the day."

Zelda set the glasses on the tiny table between the two rocking chairs and dropped into the one opposite Isobel. She still wore her ranch shirt with dried water stains and the lightest scent of doggie shampoo. "Where's Cash?"

"Zip-lining," Isobel said with a shudder. Even the thought of dangling from a cable over a cavern made her mildly nauseated. She preferred her feet steady on the ground.

"Well, that explains why you're here instead of hanging out with him," Zelda said with a good-natured laugh. She always had been one to pivot conversations to the topic of others when possible. "You and Cash were mighty snuggly on the dance floor last night."

"We had a lot to talk about before he leaves." Neither of them seemed to know how to handle the chemistry that still simmered. Perhaps it always had, but it was all the more complicated now that they'd acted up on those feelings.

"So, he's still going?" Zelda paused to pour chardonnay into each of the crystal glasses.

"Of course. He has a job. This was always just a vacation for him."

"Hmmm…" Zelda mused while sipping her drink. "Are you going to be all right when he heads out?"

"Lottie will miss him—I will too." The admission threatened to kick a hole in the wall around her emotions. She reached for her glass, sipping, needing to divert attention from her own complicated life. "So, what's the scoop with you and the cowboy?"

"No scoop," Zelda said smartly, kicking off her sneakers and wriggling her toes in her socks. "And why do you ask?"

Isobel pondered how much to say. She didn't like people prying into her life, but maybe Zelda wanted to share. Then if her sister told her to back off, Isobel would. "Rumors are floating around that there've been sparks between the two of you."

"Sparks, huh? Let's put it this way." She set aside her glassware carefully. "There's an attraction, but there's no interest in pursuing it. For either of us."

Zelda avoided her eyes a little too pointedly. More of that pivoting focus elsewhere?

"Won't that make it hard to work around each other?" As difficult as it was saying goodbye to Cash, the unresolved tension between them was tough as well. Not that her sister's love life was any of her business. Isobel reached for her glass, wondering if perhaps she was guilty of pivoting away from addressing her own issues as well.

A family trait, apparently.

"It's a big ranch." Zelda toyed with the end of her lengthy braid, a purple ribbon threaded through. "With some of the mountain magic, our feet should travel different paths so we never have to run into one another."

Maybe Isobel needed some of that Moonlight Ridge enchantment to untangle her own life. She sank back further in her rocker, eyeing the trail that led from their trio of cabins. Maybe she'd subconsciously chosen to work out here so she would catch a glimpse of Cash returning up that same path. "Do you think Gran ever walked these woods with her high school sweetheart?"

Would they get the answers they needed for Gran and for Lottie? The big donor drive was only two days away.

"I like to think she was happy and in love here back in those days." Zelda reached for her glass again, cradling it in her hands. "Being here makes me feel closer to her. Stronger somehow."

Stronger? What had she missed about Zelda's life during their time apart? "I've never thought of you as anything other than fierce."

"Here, in this place, I am myself again," Zelda said, her voice soft, low, before her face brightened and she lifted her glass. "Let's toast to new beginnings for the Dalton girls and closure for Gran's past."

Those goals felt just out of reach to Isobel, like the flowers lining the other side of the white picket fence. White blossoms tossed about by the mountain breeze. She'd made such a mess of her past with Colin, now with Cash. For heaven's sake, she couldn't even sort out the rest of this blog. What made her think she could tackle a fresh start?

She could only continue to put one foot in front of the other, going through the motions. Hoping that somehow she would find the answers needed to save her child and restore order to her life. "Cheers."

As their glasses clinked, Isobel stared into the woods, the pine trees reaching toward the sky, and she couldn't ignore that a part of her still ached to see Cash walking up the path. Back to her. A fruitless thought, a futile wish that would only bring both of them more confusion.

Confusion she could ill afford right now. Her focus had to stay firmly on safeguarding her daughter's health.

Cash was running out of things to do to keep his distance from Isobel since their night of dancing. Zip-lining may have been a little too obvious an avoidance.

For now, at least, they had a common task to keep themselves occupied as they organized their flyers and data for tomorrow's donor drive at the summer festival. Nothing would keep him from pitching in to help Lottie.

Cash sat on one side of the kitchen table, Isobel across from him. Between them, like a security wall of sorts, they organized piles of flyers, contact forms and little keychains with the website for the national donor registry. His cell phone played country tunes to fill the awkward silence.

An attempt to distract from the fact they were completely alone in the cabin.

Lottie was off at a children's music workshop. He should be celebrating how Isobel was becoming more comfortable allowing Lottie to attend events that didn't require parental presence, and the little girl was thriving with her ever-expanding world.

Cash trifolded the brochures, one after the other, taking comfort in the monotony of routine. The growing stack offered a tangible sign he was accomplishing *something*.

Isobel secured pens to five clipboards, her dark hair sliding forward as she leaned to reach into the box under the table. She came back up with two boxes of cookies individually wrapped. "Want to sample one?"

The O'Briens had donated dog paw cookies in honor of Cocoa to accompany brochures explaining the laws governing service animals. "No thanks. I snuck two already. They're Top Dog top notch, as expected."

Beyond helping Lottie, the O'Briens stated they hoped this might also increase the national donor base and local blood donations. Dr. Barnett would be present to oversee blood typing and other data needed to begin the process. They'd even donated a prime spot for their booth, right at the entrance. The O'Briens had been beyond generous in their support.

Isobel and Lottie were in good hands when he left.

His hand twitched, sliding the fold off-kilter.

Isobel wrapped a rubber band around the service animal brochures. "Thanks for your help. Please don't feel obligated to hang out here all morning. I know you wanted to check out Troy Shaw's big roping demo."

"This is more important," he said without hesitation, feeling a little guilty for the way he'd avoided her. What if he'd missed a crucial opportunity to help her?

He hadn't even been baking cookies.

"You can do both the demo and pitch in here. It's not either or." She tucked the brochures into a Rubbermaid container. "You've already been a tremendous help this morning. I can handle the rest until my sisters arrive."

He missed their old easy camaraderie. Would it be

easier when he left? Or would the gaping void inside him swallow him whole? "Are you asking me to leave?"

"Of course not," she said curtly, then scrubbed a hand over her face. "I didn't mean to snap. It's hard not to get my hopes up, but what if we're putting in all this work for nothing? What if I've taken your last weeks of recuperating?"

He dragged his chair over closer, pushing aside the shoebox filled with brochures between them. "We've been over this."

"I know." She fidgeted with the rubber band, snapping it again and again on the colorful paper. "Things are just...awkward, and I hate that. I feel like I've depended on you too much, which has kept me from being an independent mother to my child."

He wasn't quite sure what to do with that statement. Was she cutting him out of Lottie's life too? He settled for a simple answer, a truthful one. "No need to feel bad. I offered. Not because I thought you couldn't handle it but because I wanted to. You always manage, and I have no doubt that you would have tackled the mountain drive."

"Thanks for the vote of confidence." Her blue-green eyes went dewy with sentimentality—and resignation. "But our deal was that you enjoy the free vacation here. I saw that you'd circled a couple of events on today's calendar. I wish I'd seen your notes before I mentioned setting up for the donor event."

So she *was* trying to get rid of him. And that stung more than a little. Although it only made sense that she would need to start distancing herself in hopes of making the goodbye easier. That had to be the reason.

In a last-ditch attempt at a conversation like they would have had in the past, he placed a hand over hers, stopping the snapping before he asked, "And what would you circle on the daily events for yourself? Not just something to get me playing with goats?"

Her gaze held his, searching, her hand unmoving until she finally moistened her lips and eased her fingers away. "I have plenty of time here to explore—the whole summer in fact. My sisters can help me with Lottie. I'll be fine."

Hadn't he been concerned about how she would manage after he left? Well, she was making it loud and clear not to give that a second thought.

Time to quit dancing around the real issue between them. There was no ignoring that the tension had started after they had sex, a memorable night he would never forget.

"My offering to help isn't meant as pressure to sleep together again." The words fell out before he'd even fully thought through the wisdom of saying them. He definitely could have been more diplomatic.

Her head snapped back, her blue-green eyes wide. "I, uh, didn't assume any such thing. I know you better than that."

Thank goodness. He didn't want to believe he'd misread her that badly. "Then what's going on?"

She rolled her hand back and forth over a row of pens flat on the oak table for a few seconds before scooping the lot up and placing them in a cup with a heavy sigh. "I hate that sex has made things awkward between us," she blurted. "I hate even more that I don't know what to do about it. And from what I can see, you don't have a clue either."

Fair estimation. Had he pushed to be with her this afternoon, hoping she would have an answer since he didn't? They'd reached an impasse.

One thing was for certain, he wasn't going to keep torturing himself by hanging around, wanting her, knowing it couldn't lead anywhere. And he took full responsibility for that failing.

To keep from reaching for her again and making things worse between them, he shoved back his chair and stood. "You're right. We're only making things harder for ourselves. Maybe it's best I spend some time away this afternoon."

As he made fast tracks to the door, he couldn't help but hope with every step away from her that she would call out to him and ask him back.

Zelda had really, really intended to go to the pot-pourri making workshop. But she'd had to walk by the stables. Next thing she knew, her feet were detouring into the small arena.

Both wide doors were open invitingly, after all.

The cheers of the spectators drifted along the summer breeze, all the more enticement to check out Troy Shaw's lasso demo. She didn't venture all the way inside, instead lingering in the gaping opening. Half in. Half out. A noncommittal stance. She leaned against the frame, likely not even noticeable as she watched.

No question about it, he owned the ring as he went through his moves on horseback and off. He sailed the rope through the air, creating shapes and aerial maneuvers that defied gravity. Half the time, he wasn't even looking at the loop, rather entertaining the crowd with his commentary.

And all without ever once losing his Stetson. His broad shoulders stretched the plaid shirt. But then she'd drooled over those shoulders more than once. Today her gaze was drawn to his lean hips in denim and chaps.

Beyond his good looks and hot body, the man had charisma in spades. The mere sight of him sent tingles through her, the kind she hadn't felt in far too long. Thank goodness he was arrogant, so it was easier to resist him. That didn't mean, though, that she couldn't keep watching him from a distance. For his entire show, mesmerizing her so that her feet stayed planted even through the stable manager—Eliza—showing off her barrel racing skills on her quarter horse Cricket. Eliza and the sleek brown animal moved as one to the delight of the onlookers.

"Hello there," Troy's deep voice rumbled over Zelda's shoulder.

She spun on her sneaker heel, surprised she'd been so dazed she hadn't even noticed him make his way outside. He must have circled around.

Not that it mattered how he'd gotten here. In front of her. Wide-shouldered and better-looking than any human had a right to be.

The more important question? How long had she been standing here gawking at him? She swallowed down the lump in her throat and willed her hormones to simmer down. "Great show. Everyone seemed to really enjoy themselves."

Cheers and applause still rumbled from inside, although the grounds outside were nearly deserted. Just her. The cowboy. And a few grazing horses in the pasture minding their own business.

"Thanks, Miss Zelda. But they were an easy crowd to impress," he drawled before looking back over her shoulder. "Where's your niece? I didn't see her come here with you."

So he'd noticed *her* watching him. Zelda's heart lurched. "Lottie's at a music workshop being led by Raise the Woof over in one of the other barns."

"Sounds fun." He leaned back against the planked outdoor wall of the arena. "They're a talented bunch."

Zelda basked in the sound of his bourbon rich voice, all the while knowing she should go. Should. And she would. Soon. "I hope they're prepared. Lottie's a bit tone deaf."

His lopsided smile pushed a dimple into his weathered, tanned cheek. "Then I'm sure they'll have plenty of percussion instruments on hand."

A faint hint of music carried on the wind along with the distant whinny of horses and the bleating of goats from the petting zoo.

When Troy didn't make a move to leave, she nodded toward the arena, where Eliza was sparring with the rodeo clown. "I'm surprised to see her—the stable manager—here. I thought Eliza was in the band. But then I've met so many new people the past couple of weeks, I could be mixing them up."

Such a simple conversation but easy somehow, and so very different from their prickly past encounters.

"The band actually has a flexible number of members. Some positions are even doubled up. That way everyone in the group doesn't have to miss work for an event—it makes scheduling easier." As he leaned back, Troy braced one boot on the wall, his dusty chaps making her fingers itch to test the texture. His big rodeo champ belt buckle gleamed in the afternoon sun. "The band has even tapped me to join in on occasion over the summer."

Was there anything this man couldn't do? When they were handing out attributes in heaven, he'd stood in more than his fair share of lines.

"What do you play?" she asked, half expecting him to rattle off half an orchestra's worth of instruments.

"The harmonica." His grin broadened, his eyes sheepish as if embarrassed for some reason.

There was a story in there somewhere. She was sure. And curious to know someday.

"A man of many talents." Not what she'd expected, but it fit his whole sexy cowboy vibe. A vibe she would be wise to resist. "Well, I should let you get back to your adoring fans."

Troy clasped her arm lightly to stop her. "Do you have a minute more?"

"Uh, sure," she agreed, her voice far too breathy for her peace of mind. But after ogling him for the last half hour, his touch left her all the more unsteady.

"Thanks," he said, releasing her arm, his hand trailing away. Clearing his throat, he hooked his thumbs in his belt loops, his weathered face taking on that sheepish air again. "I owe you an apology. I'm sorry for being brusque, cutting you off the other day when my daughter came by."

Okay, but she didn't remember him being abrupt at all. She recalled hightailing it out of there, unsettled by the attraction to him. Not that she intended to admit as much.

So instead, she opted for a benign answer. "Her name is Harper, right?"

"Yeah." Nodding, he studied his dusty boots with undue attention. "She's having a tough time since her mom walked out on us."

Even as she willed herself not to feel sorry for him, Zelda's heart squeezed in sympathy for his daughter. "That's rough. I'm sorry—for both of you."

"I'm focused on getting her leveled out." His gaze rose again, meeting hers full-on, steely and determined.

She blinked fast. Had he thought she was hitting on him? Her cheeks heated with embarrassment. "Of course you are. As a father should be."

"Let me clarify." He scratched along his collarbone. "I just don't want you to take it personally that I wasn't returning your interest."

The heat of embarrassment morphed to outright anger. "My what?"

To think she'd almost felt sorry for him long enough to forget his arrogance. She perched her hands on her hips and stood nose to nose with him. Well, almost, since she had to look up so far.

"Uh, pardon me if I misread things." He held up his hands defensively, his palms strong and callused and very close to her shoulders. "It just seems you've been showing up with your niece quite often and then today without her. I need to be clear I'm not—"

"Not what?" she asked tightly, mighty close to stomping off. Only curiosity held her still a moment longer.

His sigh was long and heavy, caressing her cheeks with a phantom kiss. "I'm making a mess of things."

"That's an understatement." Her pride was still stinging, and she searched for a way to turn this around. To save face. And walk away with her dignity in place. "In fact, the reason I came here today was to tell you people are gossiping about the two of us. And we need to put a stop to it."

There. That made for a decent, face-saving cover story since it was true that people were talking, even if that wasn't her reason for hanging out at the arena like some buckle bunny.

His mouth went tight. "I couldn't agree with you more. The last thing I need is gossip that I'm hooking up with a Top Dog staff member."

All righty then. And that was about all her pride could take for one day. Without a word, she spun away, ready to make fast tracks to anywhere else on this ranch. Except no more than two steps later, she stepped into a gopher hole. Her arms flailed as she began falling forward.

"Careful there," Troy cautioned, fast on his feet to catch her.

"I'm fine," she bit out, scrambling to find her footing without much success.

Then his strong arms shot out to loop around her waist, hefting her up as if she weighed less than nothing. She leaned back into the hard muscled wall of his chest. The scent of leather and sweat seeped into her every breath as he eased her to her feet and turned her to face him.

She grabbed his shoulders, steadying herself as they stood chest to chest. The warmth of him radiated through her work shirt, launching a fresh wash of heat through her veins. Was it her imagination, or had his heart rate kicked up a notch? Hers sure had.

His eyes were the most beautiful shade of amber. She hadn't noticed that before and now she couldn't look away. His hands clenched tighter around her arms. She wasn't sure who moved closer first, but his mouth was brushing hers. Ever so slightly and ever so intense at the same time.

Too much for such a simple kiss.

Her heart hammering, Zelda tore herself away from him, holding up a hand to forestall any words from his arrogant mouth. With all the dignity she could muster, she strode past him toward the lodge—far away from Troy Shaw—her coworker for the rest of the summer.

She should have trusted her instincts about him rather than letting herself be drawn in by his cute cowboy butt. She definitely shouldn't have let herself be reeled in by his sad sack story about being a devoted father. Too think she'd been fool enough to Google him. She'd seen all the buzz about his reputation with women but figured that must be tabloid fluff.

Well, one thing was for certain. Moments like that weren't going to help stop the rumor mill. And she had no intentions of seeing her face with his in a gossip rag.

Chapter Fifteen

Catching up on emails and messages, Isobel waited on a bench outside the barn where Lottie was finishing up her music workshop. In the past she would have texted back and forth with Cash to kill the time, silly and frivolous exchanges that made her laugh. He'd always had a way of lifting her spirits during difficult times. She'd thought she offered the same to him.

Now they were distant and awkward, marking time until he left. Somewhat like her marriage had felt at the end, although somehow so much worse for reasons she couldn't define.

A cluster of guests bustled past—a church group according to their matching T-shirts—and she tucked her feet out of their way, further under the bench as they headed toward the petting zoo. Music drifted from inside the barn, a mix of accomplished musicians and less on-beat sounds from the younger participants putting their full effort behind the cacophony.

This day was long, with bedtime still too long away. The afternoon sun dipped lower, tucking into the V of two mountains. Cabins speckled one side, a glamping area nestled off to another with the quaintest restored vintage RVs. What would it have been like to visit here as a vacationer only with Cash and Lottie?

Isobel's phone vibrated in her hand with an incoming call. Her heart leapt at the possibility that Cash might be calling her now, that somehow they would go back to the way things were before. If he'd attended the roping demo, it would be finishing up right about now. In fact, people were already trickling by from the direction of the arena, fanning off in different directions.

A glance at the screen, though, and her heart sank with disappointment. The number? Her ex.

Sighing, she tucked the earbud in and accepted the call. "Hello, Colin. Lottie's not available right now. But I can have her phone you back."

"Actually, I need to speak with you." His familiar voice buzzed through the earpiece.

"About what?" she asked, short on patience and energy for drama right now. "I only have a minute though. Lottie's workshop will be over soon."

Colin cleared his throat three times in succession, a nervous tic of his. "I'll get straight to the point then. I'm working on my route, and I think I can swing one of my long hauls through there for a couple of days."

"Lottie would love that," she said cautiously. Her daughter would be thrilled. Isobel just hoped disappointment wouldn't follow.

"And what about you?"

She ignored the implication, pausing as a couple raced past making gestures like a lasso toss. Had they attended Troy's demo? "I can stay with one of my sisters in their cabin so you can have run of the place with Lottie."

Isobel couldn't stop herself from searching the faces for a sign of Cash. Could that be him in the distance? Her mouth went dry and her heart picked up speed.

"So, it's okay for you and Cash to play house with my child," Colin said tightly, "but you and I can't both be there for our kid."

A guilty fire flamed her cheeks while searching for a glimpse of Cash, and she tore her gaze away from the direction of the arena.

"Colin, that's not the point and you know it." She dragged in a steadying breath to keep from losing her temper. Irritation nipped all the same. She sat up straighter, her sneakers rasping along loose gravel. "Furthermore, we're divorced. As I've told you before, you have no right to dictate who I spend my time with."

"Fine," he snapped. "I won't come then."

His words were like a stab to her heart as she remembered so many times he'd let Lottie down. And, yes, let her down as well. Her anger picked up steam even as she kept her voice low. "Do not take out your anger at me on our child. That's petty. You know I have always, always given you unlimited access to our daughter."

The cell line crackled for a moment, with only the sound of traffic from his end, then a belabored sigh echoed. "Well, I'll see what I can work out."

She knew that petulant tone in his voice too well. He wasn't coming. And that act of selfishness, utter lack of understanding just how much his child needed to see him angered her to the roots of her hair and the tips of her toes.

Over the years, she had done her best to be fair, to give Colin every opportunity possible to be the father Lottie deserved. And she would continue to do so, but right now, she was heartsick and weary from dealing with her ex-husband's immaturity.

"Colin, I've got a poor connection." She tapped the phone repeatedly—childish in her own way too. "You know how bad cell reception can be in the mountains. Text me if you're coming, and I'll make sure Lottie's available. Bye."

Disconnecting, she slumped back on the bench, her fingers gripping the cell until it bit into her skin. She wanted to scream out her frustration, to tell Colin once and for all the countless ways he'd hurt her and their child. Isobel was tired of being careful and gracious in her responses. She let her head fall to rest against the back of the bench, blinking fast to hold back the tears stinging.

"Everything okay?" Cash's voice rumbled just before he sat beside her.

No. Not even remotely. But he was the last person she wanted to speak with right now. Well, the second to last, after Colin. "I'm fine. Thank you."

"You don't look it." He angled toward her, his elbow on the back of the bench.

"It's not your problem," she said, leaning down to retrieve her purse from behind her feet. She didn't have the energy for another tense conversation. "But thank you all the same."

He eyed the phone still clutched in her hand. "Bad news?" His brows pinched together. "Was it something about Lottie?"

"She's fine. And there's no word on a donor." Isobel thought about just walking off but couldn't bring herself to be outright rude to a man who had meant so much to them both. "My ex called. He's thinking about swinging through to see Lottie."

"And you're upset about that?" He searched her eyes, his own gaze inscrutable.

"Let me clarify." She knew they would be saying their goodbyes soon, but she couldn't stomach him leaving with a poor impression of her. "I want Lottie to have a good relationship with her dad, and I don't want him to let her down again."

"What about you?" His hand dangled from the back of the bench, close to her but not touching even though in the past he might have toyed with a lock of her hair, even slid his arm around her. "How do you feel about seeing him?"

"Why would you ask that?" She thought she'd been crystal clear about her feelings for Colin—or lack thereof.

"He was your husband," Cash said, his mouth tight. "You must have loved him once. Maybe you love him still?"

What in the world was he driving at? Could he be jealous of Colin? The thought stirred a hope she couldn't risk feeling. "I absolutely do not love my exhusband. Those feelings died a long time ago."

"Then why do you have such a strong reaction to a

simple phone call from him?" Cash pulled his arm off the back of the bench and clasped his hands between his knees.

"I just told you. Because I don't want him to let down our daughter again." She could see the skepticism on his face, and it stoked her anger. And it made her wonder all the more why he was asking, but her pride wouldn't let her question him if he had feelings for her. So instead, she asked, "How would you react if your ex-girlfriend called and said she was planning a trip to Moonlight Ridge?"

He blinked, staying silent for a few heartbeats too long before saying, "It wouldn't matter to me either way."

His hesitation washed away any hint of hope, the pain all the worse so close on the heels of a call from Colin reminding her of all the ways she'd failed in the past. "Are you so sure about that? It took you a long time to answer."

His head dropped, his fingers still linked. "She walked out on me at the worst time in my life. That's not something a person gets over."

There it was. The truth of his feelings, the very thing she'd feared in the depths of her heart. Caring for a man who loved someone else. She swallowed hard, the pain of realization burning all the way to her gut. "So you're not over her."

"That isn't what I said." He tipped his face toward her, his eyebrows raised. "I meant I can't forgive her. It feels like you're diverting attention off yourself and feelings you may have for your ex."

She wasn't buying his deflection. Not for a minute. Too many times during an argument, Colin had accused her of imagining things. Cash wasn't shallow like Colin, but maybe on a subconscious level he'd been trying to fill a void in his life with her.

And she refused to be second best ever again.

"Or that you're perceiving a problem in my breakup that you're suffering from in your own. Regardless, nothing's been right between us since we slept together, and there's no going back to the way things were."

"Are you telling me to leave?" A flash of pain whispered through his eyes.

But then their friendship had meant so much to them both these past months. She hadn't imagined that part and felt an agonizing echo inside herself that only grew worse the more time they spent in this awful state of limbo.

She pressed her hands to his cheeks, his stubble rasping a gentle abrasion against her palms. "I'm saying we're both hurting by prolonging the goodbye."

Her quiet declaration hung there between them, the death knell to anything more between them.

He clasped her wrists, his forehead falling to rest against hers. "I agree. The donor drive is over tomorrow. I would like to see that through for Lottie, then I'll leave first thing in the next day. Is that okay?"

Nodding, she didn't trust herself to speak. Her voice would crack and the tears would flow. She squeezed her eyes shut and let her hands fall away, taking her time to savor this last chance to touch him.

He released her, pushed to his feet without another

word and walked away, leaving a void behind him she wasn't sure could ever be filled.

A man on a mission, Troy pushed into the ranch's gift shop. He needed to pick up a present for his teen-age daughter. One of the crystal pieces sold here would be just the ticket.

He'd upended her life by bringing her here. Even if he had the best of intentions for the long-term stability of her future, she was a teenager living in the moment, having lost her mom and her home.

No doubt, he'd made things worse by his ill-timed preoccupation with a certain Top Dog lady groomer. What had he been thinking by kissing her earlier today? Of course, that was the whole point. He hadn't thought at all. He'd just acted on impulse like the "old" Troy, a man he couldn't afford to be any longer. For Harper's sake, he had to turn his life around.

He pushed open the front door, the bell chiming his arrival in the charming little store filled with more than souvenirs. Shelves featured vintage restored toys and carved wooden animals, along with treats from Bone Appétit Bakery.

Waving aside the help of the shop manager so she could assist others, he made his way to the display table featuring crystal jewelry made from gemstones mined out of the Sulis Cave and Springs. Bypassing a tray of rings, he trailed his fingers along necklaces dangling from a long dowel. A small plaque noted credit: *Gems by River Jack*.

A pink stone set in a flower charm caught his attention. Perfect. He reached, only to have his hand collide with another.

"Sorry," he said, looking up to find… "Oh, you."

Zelda jerked back her hand as if burned—her cheeks flaming red. "Oh, uh, you too."

He jammed his hands in his pockets, blurting, "Are you following me?"

Not his most subtle statement, but she kept showing up, and he didn't want her to get the wrong idea from that impulsive kiss. He needed to put a stop to things before they spiraled out of control.

That heat on her face fired in her eyes now. "You have got to be kidding me. I'm here buying a gift for my niece. I could ask if *you* are following *me*."

Two older gentleman shopping by the carved cigar boxes shot disapproving stares his way. They were right, of course. He hadn't sounded very gentlemanly, and he didn't need the gossip.

Troy stepped around the display table, his shoulders blocking the rest of the store from watching their conversation. "Sorry," he said softly. "It just seems… suspicious that you're here."

Zelda jabbed him in the chest with one finger. "Listen up, Mr. Cowboy Ego. I am not following you." She poked again for each point. "I'm not trying to pin you down and steal your ever lovin' freedom because of one silly kiss. It didn't mean any more to me than it did to you."

Finished, she folded her arms over her chest. Her very pretty chest, gentle curves only inches away.

Eyes up. "Zelda, I apologize for that moment—"

"That kiss."

"Fine," he said through gritted teeth. "Yes, that kiss. I'm not sure what came over me."

"My undeniable charms, no doubt." Her smile was slow and dark with irony.

"This isn't funny," he hissed, glancing behind him to make sure no one overheard. "I was here looking for a gift for my daughter since I've been so busy this week. I'm a single dad with no time for a fling."

"A fling? Excuse me? I'm not interested in a *fling*, especially not with *you*. Let's both forget it ever happened." She extended a hand. "Deal?"

The air hung heavy between them with charged emotions, from their sparring and kiss. His chest pumped faster as he hauled in deep breaths filled with the scent of nearby candles and *her*.

This woman was a dangerous temptation he could ill afford. Troy clasped her hand in his, steeling himself to ignore the skin-to-skin sensation. "Deal."

Pivoting away hard and fast, he hightailed it out of the gift shop and into the late-day foot traffic. Only to realize that he'd been so caught up in seeing Zelda, he'd forgotten all about buying Harper a necklace. Time to get his priorities back in order.

From this point going forward, he would do his level best to make sure he and Zelda Dalton crossed paths as little as possible.

Cash wondered how many miles he would have to hike, how much mountain air he would have to breathe before he cleared his head from his argument with Isobel? Except it was worse than a fight. It had been a heartrending goodbye.

Their friendship had been so strong during such troubled times that he would have wagered nothing could tear it apart. He'd been wrong.

Worst of all, he'd seen the hurt in her eyes and knew he'd put it there. The guilt seared him through and through until he accepted there was nothing he could do except honor her request to leave.

One foot in front of the other, he trudged up the narrow mountain path, hoping he could walk off the stress before the threat of rain clouds overhead forced him to turn around. He braced one hand along the rock wall on his right, his left side offering a breathtaking view of the valley that once would have held him spellbound. Now its beauty left him cold.

How could he have let things spiral so out of control with Isobel? Leaving her and Lottie had been difficult enough when they were on a positive footing, but now? Saying goodbye would slice away a piece of his heart.

Stopping, he slumped back against the jagged rock and braced his hands on his knees, his heart slugging with grief. He'd come here with such hopes for healing for Lottie's body. For Isobel's heart. And yes, for his own soul as well.

None had been accomplished.

He wanted to rage at the mountain and fate for all he'd lost. The infamous Moonlight Ridge magic was total bunk, nothing but a fairy tale. Certainly there was none left for him and for Isobel.

But as long as there could be enough to give Lottie

the miracle she needed, he would consider the heartache worthwhile.

The breeze kicked up around him, stirring leaves and the reminder he should head back before nightfall. Faster still, the wind swirled until he could swear it whistled upward from the drop-off below the path.

The whistling intensified until he realized it wasn't just the breeze. Rather, the wind carried the voice of child crying out, "Help me. Is there somebody up there?"

Cash straightened, tipping his head toward the sound. "Hello? Hello? Can you hear me?"

"Yes!" a little boy's voice screamed. "Yes, I'm down here! I fell and I need help!"

"I hear you!" Cash shouted, old work instincts firing to life inside him, focused on locating the child. "Keep talking so I can follow your voice."

"My name is Sebastian Johnson," he rambled, high pitched and panicked. "I'm seven years old."

"Sebastian?" Cash called, continued up the path toward the voice. Lottie's little friend was down there? How many times had Cash witnessed the boy running after his sisters, shouting for them to wait up? "Is anyone down there with you?" He kept his voice level, calm, just as he'd done in so many rescue scenarios on the job, even when his instincts roared that the odds were low. Like the fire that had killed Elijah. "Are you hurt?"

No sign of the boy yet. He scanned harder, until he detected a slight break in the lush green, like some branches had been broken off.

"My ankle hurts really bad, Mr. Cash," he said, his words wobbly, softer, coming from the direction of that parting in the foliage. "I can't stand up. Are you coming? Please don't leave me."

"I'm coming, buddy." He stretched out on his stomach and looked over the edge, scanning over the dense undergrowth until…yes…he spotted a flash of red. He squinted for a better look, wishing he had binoculars. "Sebastian? What color are your clothes? Can you wave to me?"

"Red, my shirt is red, and I'm wearing blue jeans," he said just as his tiny hand slid past a cluster of vines waving weakly.

Squinting, Cash could just make out the shape of a small child huddled on a ledge. A very tiny ledge. One that wouldn't support a second person. Any rescue would need to be attempted by lowering down with a rope, staying suspended over the boy. Tricky, to say the least, and that didn't even take into account the muddy path that had already given way once when the kid first fell.

"I see you, Sebastian," he called out, inching his phone from his back pocket. "I'm calling for help."

"Don't go," the little boy cried, his voice getting fainter. "Please don't leave me."

"I'm not." He tried to reassure the child while dialing his cell, the phone ringing. Relief pumped through him. "I'll stay here with you until help arrives."

He hoped.

His call to the ranch's front desk dropped. As did the next. His battery life diminished with each effort. Before long, he would have none left at all, and he would be faced with the unimaginable decision of whether to stay or leave Sebastian while going back for help.

Frustration had him grinding his teeth and easing back from the edge to sit on the path to check the device. His cell only had one bar of connectivity.

Maybe a text would make it through? Thumbs flying, Cash dashed off a message to Jacob O'Brien, praying it would send, his heart hammering. He dropped a pin with his location as well.

He waited and waited until the screen showed it had delivered. He swallowed down the lump of relief. "Keep talking to me, Sebastian. Sing your ABCs if you can't think of anything else."

As the child warbled his ABCs, followed by the birthday song, Cash continued to type out pleas for assistance to others in case Jacob was away from his phone. He messaged Isobel, then Hollie O'Brien, sending his location to each. Waiting for at least one of them to respond to confirm help was on the way.

Much longer and he would have to leave Sebastian and go back to the ranch for assistance. "Sebastian? Are you still with me, buddy?"

Silence, other than chirps from the rustling of branches. Was that a raindrop? Or just sap from a tree?

"Sebastian?" Flat on his stomach again, Cash peered over the edge of the cliff where he'd seen the red shirt. Rocks skittered from beneath him, rolling into the brush below.

A ping echoed from his phone. From an incoming

text. He snatched up his cell from the ground to find an incoming message from Jacob. A sigh of relief flooded through him.

Jacob: Got your message. Sebastian Johnson was reported missing by his parents. Help on the way. R u ok to stay with him?

Cash: Yes. Earth is wet and unstable. No room on ledge with kid. Sebastian injured a foot. Rain threatening. Need ropes.

"Sebastian," Cash called out again, hoping the child could hear him even if he didn't respond, "help is on the way. Hang on. Okay? Answer me."

"Mr. Cash," the wobbly voice pleaded. "I'm really scared."

Everything inside Cash screamed to scale down the mountainside and assist the boy. After all, the firefighter training included basic medical care. But without at least a rope to secure himself, he could end up doing more harm than good by dislodging more of the muddy, unstable earth.

"Kiddo, hang in there, I'm right here." He searched for the right words to reassure the young boy in such a terrifying moment. Panic could be devastating for the child. If he moved and dislodged himself, the rest of the drop wasn't survivable.

Professional instincts began to go up in flames. Then, from the far recesses of his memory, Cash could hear Isobel's voice as she shared about her grandmother.

About the stories and magical healing of Moonlight Ridge. And Cash knew exactly what to say next.

"Sebastian, listen up. I'm going to tell you a tale about the way miracles happen around this mountain…"

Chapter Sixteen

Normally manicures were relaxing. But Isobel's stress level had gone way past anything an hour in a nail salon could fix. Still, she went through the motions for her sisters and Lottie, their chatter swirling around her as she watched the technician create puppy paw art over the pink base.

After her awful argument with Cash, Isobel just wanted to lock herself in her room and cry into her pillow for days on end. But she'd promised this outing to Lottie, and her daughter was already nervous about the big donor event at the summer festival tomorrow, worried rain might keep people from attending. Isobel couldn't guarantee success at the event, but she could keep this vow.

Hopefully without bursting into tears before the polish dried.

The ranch had a small spa in a cabin, more earthy than chic, with a cedar sauna, hot stone massages and four manicure chairs. Bottles of polish lined one shelf, others filled with essential oils and small jars of bath salts, their aroma overriding any acetone scent. This must be what heaven smelled like. Except she was too miserable to enjoy it because she'd lost her best friend and she had only herself to blame.

"Look, Mommy," Lottie called out from the neighboring chair, "she painted flowers on my fingernails."

"That's beautiful, sweetie." Isobel forced a smile on her face. "Did you thank Aunt Neve for treating us to manicures?"

"Thank you, Aunt Neve." Lottie blew a kiss with her dry hand. "You're great. I love you to the moon and back."

Neve waggled her fingers, her nails blue, each with a different tiny bird. "Love you too, sweetie. We'll be all prettied up for the summer festival tomorrow."

Isobel blinked back the threat of tears and went through the motions of being social. How long before she would feel like herself again?

"Zelda," Isobel said, glancing over at her middle sister soaking her feet in a pedicure tub, "what did you choose?"

"All different colors so I don't have to decide." Zelda had bypassed a mani since dog grooming was tough on her nails. She certainly appeared wrung out from work, with dark circles under her eyes.

Concern nudged past her own heartache as Isobel slid her fingers under the dryer. "Are you okay? You look, uh, distracted."

"Just a long, irritating afternoon." Zelda chewed her thumbnail for moment before blurting, "Troy Shaw gets on my very last nerve and it's not like I can avoid him. Although, going forward, I intend to do my level best to make sure our paths cross as little as possible."

Eyes narrowing, Neve sat up straighter while keeping her hands still. "Is he hassling you? I've heard he has quite a reputation with women."

Two of the nail technicians glanced up with interest at the potential gossip. The way rumors spread around this small community, she wondered how Gran's secret could be so difficult to crack.

Zelda shook her head, her fat braid swishing emphatically. "He's just irritating. Arrogant. But nothing I can't handle."

Man trouble seemed to be contagious these days. Although Zelda seemed to have her situation under control, while Isobel could barely breathe, her heart hurt so badly. Would this pain ease after Cash left? Right now, she couldn't imagine how as she already missed him with every breath.

Her cell phone vibrated on the table by her UV light nail dryer. She ignored the notice. But then it buzzed again and again. Frowning, she angled to check on the incoming texts—from Cash. Strange. She eased one hand free and tapped the screen, careful not to ruin her nails.

Cash: Young boy slipped off a path. Sebastian Johnson. Tumbled down cliff. Injured foot. Don't know how bad. Send help to this location ASAP.

Her hand gravitated to her mouth in horror. She'd wanted a distraction, but not this.

Another text vibrated through.

Cash: I'm staying with the boy. Will climb down to give aid if necessary, but ground soft. Don't want to risk dislodging him.

Isobel shot to her feet and jammed her phone into her pocket. "Sorry, but I have to leave." She started to explain, then saw the concern in Lottie's eyes. She didn't want to worry her child. Isobel took a screenshot of Cash's text's and sent it to her sisters. "Here are the details. Could you watch Lottie for me until I return?"

Zelda took one look at her phone, her eyes going wide. "Oh, my. Of course. I'll reach out to Jacob and Hollie to make sure they're on their way as well. You should be careful with your cell battery."

"Thank you," Isobel gasped out, backing toward the door, sidestepping Cocoa and a rolling cart full of towels.

Neve waved Isobel away. "We're fine. Go do whatever is needed. Keep us posted when you can."

Lottie chewed her bottom lip. "Mommy? What's wrong?"

"Cash is helping find a lost little boy, and he needs help." Hoping the simplified answer would be enough, she pressed a quick kiss on top of her daughter's head. "I'll be back before you know it."

As she raced across the salon, she pulled up the message again, opening the location pin and smacking a hand against the glass door on her way out. Running there would be faster than retrieving her van and driving. She would have to walk the path anyway.

Her mind spinning with horrifying scenarios of Cash

in harm's way on that mountain, she placed a call to Hollie making sure the ranch staff had been notified. On autopilot, she raced past the gift shop, then Bone Appétit, then by the firepit on her way toward the correct path leading away from the stables.

Up a mountain.

She didn't even hesitate. No fear or vertigo was greater than her need to reach Cash and poor little Sebastian. Lottie would be upset once she learned about her friend.

And Cash. Isobel couldn't bear the thought something might happen to him as he pulled off a heroic rescue with no thought to his own safety. He'd only just recovered from the fire and hadn't yet healed from the trauma of losing his friend.

How would he cope if the worst happened today with the child? So many tragic possibilities spiraled through her head. Her imagination was a blessing at work, but it was a curse right now.

Her phone continued to light up with notifications, updates from Hollie that Jacob was heading out with ropes and a first aid kit. The fire department in Moonlight Ridge had been contacted as well and would arrive as soon as possible.

Her heart hammered faster with fear and exertion, she drew in one ragged breath after another. Eyes focused front on the path. No looking left or right. Definitely no looking down.

Rocks skittered from under her feet. She lurched forward and just managed to grab a tree branch to keep from face-planting. The world wobbled in front of her, the whole valley spreading out in a panorama that left her queasy.

Swallowing down bile, she righted herself. Strengthened her resolve. Cash had been so alone after the fire, no one to support him. She didn't know what she could do to help, but holding back and watching the world come to the rescue wasn't an option.

Grasping one branch after another, she continued her climb until she heard Cash's voice in the distance. Her heart leapt with hope and something stronger, more than friendship.

The path took a sharp turn around a corner and she saw him. Isobel sagged against the rock wall with relief, her knees threatening to buckle. She gave herself a moment to catch her breath and soak in the sight of him.

He lay flat on his stomach, his head over the edge as he spoke to Sebastian. His reassuring voice rumbled down toward the stranded child. His words took shape, and she realized he was telling Sebastian a variation of one of her grandmother's stories. He didn't have the details all correct, but the gist of the tale was unmistakable.

A boy and his dog had wandered into a cave and had become lost. The child was scared and alone, shivering in the damp of the cavern until three fairy sisters sprinkled their magical leaves to light the way home.

An avalanche of emotions swept over her, more than just nostalgia for Gran. More than simply fear for her own child transferring to this young boy. She no longer flinched from naming the feeling filling every corner of her being.

She was overwhelmed with love for Cash, a man full of heart and vulnerability. A man who had been hurt by life as she had. Yet he still gave of himself to help others.

He was a shining example of what a brave and vulnerable man should be. So much more so than Colin had ever been. Instead of questioning Cash and pushing him away out of fear, she should have celebrated the gift of having him in her life. But she'd learned from her mistakes.

Time to face her anxieties and embrace life full-on. She would do whatever it took—face whatever fears life threw at her—for a chance to make things right with Cash, a man who filled her heart and life with love.

Cash kept his focus zeroed in on that patch of red below where Sebastian curled up on a tiny ledge. They'd worked out a system where every time the word *mountain* came up in the story, the child would call out. He'd picked up the trick at one of Lottie's story times. The librarian had commented it helped her monitor the children's engagement.

"And that's how magic found its way to the Moonlight Ridge *mountains*," Cash finished.

"Mountains," Sebastian chanted back. "I'm g-g-getting c-c-cold."

From shock? Or the setting sun? Neither was good. Cash couldn't dodge the sense that time was running out.

And just as he was about to give up and start the trek back down the mountain, he felt the weight of a gaze behind him. Careful to keep his movements measured and slow, he glanced over his shoulder, expecting to find Jacob.

Instead, he saw Isobel leaning against the rock wall, pale and gripping the jagged edges for dear life. He'd texted her to send for help, never expecting she would make the climb up to this steep altitude. He didn't have time to read into her actions. Not now. Later he would ponder.

Right now, only Sebastian mattered. "Is Jacob on his way?"

"I know others are on their way." She inched closer, her back still to the wall. "But I didn't want to wait around while they gathered supplies. I ran straight over in case there was something I could do now."

He would have chuckled if the situation wasn't so dire. Mountain rescue wasn't exactly up her alley, but seeing her here…he should have known. When others were in need, Isobel never flinched. Her grit was mesmerizing.

"Cash?" The shout from Jacob echoed up the path. "Are you still there?"

"Up here," Cash shouted. "Isobel too."

"Thank heaven," Jacob sighed, his voice growing closer. "Troy's with me as well."

A moment later, the two men eased round the corner into sight, Troy with ropes looped over his shoulder and Jacob carrying a large first aid kit.

They still had a monumental task ahead of them, but at least he could send Isobel back to level ground. "It's okay now," Cash reassured her. "You can go."

She shook her head. "I'm staying right here until Sebastian is safe."

The jut of her chin broadcast her determination loud and clear. Fair enough. He didn't have time to question her motives. Cash pivoted toward the other two men, their heads close together as they talked, peering down at the stranded boy.

Rocks skittered, followed by a scream from Sebastian that echoed up to wrap around them all. Isobel paled, as far from the ledge as possible. She gripped the trunk of a smaller tree.

The longer they spoke, the deeper the trenches in Jacob's forehead until he shook his head in defeat. "I'm not seeing a feasible path down for anyone much bigger than a child."

Cash bit back a curse. He'd come to the same conclusion but prayed he was wrong or missed an option. "Then let me try."

Troy tucked his head low and whispered, "You're too heavy and you know it. You and the boy both would be at risk. The best bet? Wait until a helicopter can lower a basket."

Cash hissed, "Wait until morning, you mean? What if it starts raining?"

Jacob clapped him on the shoulder. "I don't like that answer any more than you do, but sending any of us three men down would be a guaranteed disaster. And it's not like we can send a child down the side to pass him a rope."

"I'll do it," Isobel said from behind them.

All the blood rushed from Cash's head, giving him

a vertigo that had nothing to do with heights. The mere thought of Isobel dangling over the edge of the cliff, coming to harm—or worse—was beyond considering.

Cash stepped closer to her and gripped her shoulders, both to steady her and to keep her from launching forward into harm's way. "We'll figure out something else."

"There isn't another option," she insisted, looking from him to the other two men. "You know I'm right. If we're going to try a rescue before dark, I'm the best bet."

One glance at Jacob and Troy confirmed they agreed with her. Troy was already fashioning the rope into loops. Jacob knelt to open the first aid kit on the ground.

"No," Cash insisted, feeling like Don Quixote tilting fruitlessly at windmills. "I can go. If I can't manage without touching the ledge, haul me up, and then we can try plan B."

Still, the men silently continued their prep with fast efficiency.

Isobel cradled his face in both her hands. "Cash, I want to help. I *need* to help. I can't ask a person to risk his or her life in a transplant surgery for my daughter yet be unwilling to put my life on the line for someone else's child," she said with tender honesty and unerring accuracy. "I have faith I'll be okay because you'll have a rope around me, and I *know* you won't let go. No matter what."

Her eyes shone with total trust that humbled him after how he'd been unable to save Elijah. He also saw her deep determination and knew she was right. This was the best way.

His throat closed up, and he could only nod even as fear raged inside him. He pressed a fierce and fast kiss to her mouth, refusing to believe it could be the last time he saw her, touched her. "Okay."

Her hand trailed along his cheek before she eased back and addressed the other men. "It's time."

Cash soaked in the sight of her as she twisted her hair back into a ponytail, out of the way. Willing his breathing and his heart into a steady pattern, he clasped one end of the rope as Troy secured the other in some convoluted web that resembled a sling and belt in one. The cowboy passed her a second looped rope for her to lower to Sebastian once she was close enough. Somehow, she would secure the child to herself with a hook as a backup. With some Moonlight Ridge luck, if the slip loop could be secured around the boy, she wouldn't have to set foot on that ledge at all.

Isobel smiled at Cash, her heart in her eyes just before she disappeared from sight over the side—a gut punch he felt all the way through.

Bracing his feet, he eased her down inch by inch. Jacob stood behind him, holding as well, but Cash's grip stayed firm. Time shifted into a surreal, dreamlike state, every second interminably long and far too fast all at once.

Hand over fist, he lowered her bit by bit. The weight of her felt so slight, scarily so, as if she might fly away. Leaves and branches rustled as she brushed past, but she didn't utter a word of complaint.

Channeling his professional instincts was harder than ever, but he refused to fail her. He would fall over the side of the cliff himself before he would let go. Could that be why he struggled so with Elijah's death? Survivor's guilt over not fighting to the death to get his friend out faster? The therapist at the rehab center had certainly brought up the possibility more than once, only Cash hadn't been ready to hear it.

He eased her lower still until dimly, he registered her call to stop. She would try to secure the rope around Sebastian without putting her weight on the ledge.

Now, as he found himself in another nightmarish life-or-death moment, faced with her incredible bravery, he saw his own cowardice. He recognized all the ways he'd held back from Isobel out of fear of failing again and faced a truth he could no longer deny.

He loved Isobel with all his heart, more than he'd cared for anyone in his life. And out of fear of being hurt if he lost her, he'd rejected his feelings. He wanted to shout his love for her into the abyss below, the sun so low he wondered how she could even see to maneuver in the murky final rays.

Every minor sway or tug on the rope sent his heart into his throat until an eternity later, she shouted, "We're ready. Pull us up."

Relief left him lightheaded. His heart rate kicked up a notch as he gathered the rope, the increased weight assuring him of both passengers, the burn against his palms a sweet reminder of success. The soothing tones of her voice drifted on the cooling breeze as she crooned to Sebastian on their way toward the edge. How calm she sounded. How in control.

Then she was in sight once again, her arms wrapped tight around Sebastian. Was there blood on her arm? Or just dirt. He forced aside distracting thoughts. As Cash kept his grip on the rope, Troy and Jacob hauled them the rest of the way onto the path, as far away from the edge as possible.

Isobel rolled to her back with a long, gusty sigh, her face pale but victorious. She was so incredible she stole his breath as surely as she'd stolen his heart.

Just as he'd held on to that rope, he knew he wasn't letting Isobel slip through his fingers ever again. Whatever it took, he would be the man she deserved and pray he was lucky enough to win her love.

He just had to find the right time and the right way to win her back.

Chapter Seventeen

The next morning after only four hours of sleep, Isobel was running on adrenaline and caffeine as she manned her booth at the summer festival. Her stomach was a mishmash of emotions: hope for Lottie, residual turmoil over the terrifying rescue and complete confusion over how to approach Cash.

If she could even find him. She snuck another glance at her phone to see if he'd texted, then returned her attention to the line forming at her booth.

Foot traffic at her table had been nonstop since the gate had opened at eight. Thank heaven for Neve's help, Dr. Barnett's too, in answering questions and passing out flyers. The librarian, Susanna, had graciously agreed to watch over Lottie, insisting it was no trouble at all, and her little boy, Benji, enjoyed the company.

Isobel had waited for this day for so long, only to have it pass in a haze, unable to rejoice with Cash over the huge turnout. She didn't even have a clue where things stood between them, and he'd already left the cabin when she'd woken up. Her love for him felt so new, her heart tender as it stretched to accommodate the fullness of her growing emotions. She ached to tell him but struggled with how to start. Never again would she chase a man who didn't want her. She might be braver than before, but she wasn't foolish.

Regardless, there hadn't been time to talk last night after rescuing Sebastian. By the time paramedics stitched up a gash on her arm—deeper than she'd wanted Cash to know when it happened—it was past midnight. Lottie had insisted on sleeping in the bed with her, needing reassurance, which was understandable. Isobel had felt more than a little unsteady as well, that little boy's close brush with death shaking her to her core. The thought of losing her child was unbearable, reminding her all over again the stakes riding on this festival.

Booths and vendor tables circled the town square, showcasing vintage toys, wood carvings, treats from the bakery and so much more. A local quilting group displayed baby blankets and restored full-size bedding. The librarian sat in a rocker with her reading buddy pup Atlas, passing out books to children. Tucked in a bower of trees, an archway had been built to resemble the Sulis Springs Cave, with lettering carved in to read, *Gems by River Jack*. An older gentleman stood inside displaying his jewelry.

But where was Cash? Had he left already? She couldn't bear the thought that he would leave without saying goodbye, no matter how awful their argument had been.

She scanned the crowds, searching for a glimpse of him. She looked past Zelda at a dog washing station and Lottie making suncatchers with her friends.

Country tunes filled the air, reminding her of that

special dance with Cash, an enchanted evening that had led to more between them. Even if she'd known how things would turn out between them, she would still take that night of making love with him. If scaling down the cliff had taught her anything, she'd learned life was short.

Then finally, she saw him over by the dais. Her heart leapt in her chest in that way she now recognized as a signal of her love for him. Cash stood by the sound system, talking with the lead singer of Raise the Woof.

A light hand on her shoulder drew her attention back to the table where Hollie waited expectantly, decked out in full cowgirl gear, complete with rhinestone boots. "Isobel, how's your arm feeling today? We were all so worried about you. I wasn't sure you'd be able to make it here today."

Since Dr. Barnett and Neve seemed to have things well under control passing out brochures and taking information, Isobel tucked back a step to speak with Hollie. Without the O'Briens, none of today's event would have been possible.

"I'm fine, Hollie, thank you for asking." Her arm throbbed and she'd lost count of the bruises, but there was no point in complaining. The day could have turned out so much worse. She sagged down onto a bale of hay. "I wouldn't miss today's event for anything."

Hollie sat beside her, clasping her hands and squeezing. "You're the hero of the day with your rescue."

"I was the right person at the right time," Isobel said, brushing aside the accolades. Besides, she'd been scared to death. "Anyone else in my shoes would have done the same."

"I beg to differ," Hollie said with a smile, her brown side braid trailing over one shoulder. "But let's not argue. I want you to know how your bravery inspired others. The story of what you did spread like wildfire, beyond just our town and into neighboring counties."

"I'm just thankful Sebastian is all right." Making suncatchers with Lottie, the little boy looked none the worse for wear from his misadventure, other than a bandage on his sprained ankle. Although his sisters standing close watch over him appeared more than a little contrite.

"Of course, that's the most important," Hollie agreed, sitting up straighter, both boots flat on the dusty ground. "But I came over here to let you know that your rescue had a direct correlation on attendance this afternoon. Our phones are ringing off the hook with people asking for details. Attendance is double what we expected. People have been telling us how they came because they wanted to be tested for Lottie's donor drive."

A flush of warmth spread through Isobel. That hadn't been her intent in helping, but relief surged through her over the increased possibility of helping her child, of solving Gran's mystery. If only she could celebrate with Cash as more than a friend, as a partner, as the love of her life. "Cash played a part in that as well by finding Sebastian, notifying help, keeping Sebastian calm."

"You two make quite a team." Hollie crossed her

arms over her fringed vest. "Are you going to let him leave without telling him how you feel?"

Isobel didn't bother denying her love for him. She suspected it was on her face for the world to see. "I won't chase a man who doesn't want me ever again."

"Are you so sure Cash doesn't want a relationship with you?"

"He told me as much in an argument right before Sebastian's accident."

"Oh," Hollie raised her eyebrows, nodding, "because people never get defensive in a fight and deny their true feelings."

Isobel's gaze gravitated back to Cash with the band. She could still hear the sound of him reassuring little Sebastian. As she thought of all the scars—outward and inward—that Cash bore, she wondered if he could ever accept the love and comfort of others.

Or would he continue to wall himself off?

But was she any better? Holding back out of fear of rejection? What did that say about the strength of her love that she flinched from exposing her feelings?

The thought of telling Cash how she felt and having him turn her away was scarier than hurtling herself off the side of a mountain. There was only one thing more frightening. Staying quiet and forever wondering what might have been. She didn't want to be like Gran, having to reconcile her regrets in a last will and testament.

Resolve filled her from head to toe, shining a light inside her that overcame the shadowy doubts. She didn't know what a future with Cash might look like since they were on such different paths.

But wherever that journey led them, she intended to take the biggest risk of her life and let Cash know how very deeply she loved him.

The evening dinner and dance party was well underway, marking an end to the first day of the summer festival.

Nerves kicked up a storm in Cash's gut as he strode into the party barn, time approaching for him to roll out his plans for Isobel. While this was the same space used for the hoedown a few days earlier, the barn sported a fancier feel, more like a wedding reception. Twinkle lights glinted overhead, along with drapes of white gauze. Live flowers decorated the standing tables, with fresh greenery and candles. Even the clothing was more formal, with women in dresses and men adding a sports jacket to go with their jeans.

The perfect setting for a summery romantic evening.

He'd been running full-out most of the day, arranging details for his grand gesture to woo Isobel. Although, the effort would have been twice as hard alone. Everywhere he looked, he saw a new friend—each a Top Dog Ranch employee—who had offered help. From the bakery chef to the landscaper to the band, even the gift shop manager.

Every time he caught a glimpse of Isobel, he ached to sweep her away, to bury his fingers in her thick brown hair and tell her how much he loved her. But the donor drive was too important for Lottie.

Even if he could have managed to part the crowd between him and Isobel's table.

A tug on his jacket drew his attention downward to find Lottie smiling up at him, Cocoa too.

"Wow, Cash," Lottie said with wide eyes, "are those flowers for my mommy?"

His hand clenched around the bouquet he held, his grip crinkling the paper wrapped around the stems of the daisies and miniature yellow roses.

"These are for you, actually." He had others for Isobel, later. But this was Lottie's big day and he wanted her to feel celebrated. "And if you look closely, there are pirate doubloons tied to the ribbon—they're chocolate."

Lottie squealed. "They're so pretty and you are the very best pirate. I think daisies are my new favorite flower. I'm going to put them in a glass of water on the table so they stay alive until we go."

"That's a smart idea."

"Thanks. I do all my homework and try to be my very best." She toyed with the bow and mesh bag of chocolate coins for a moment before asking, "Are you leaving tomorrow? You won't go without saying goodbye to me, will you?"

His heart squeezed as he thought of all the times her father had let her down, Isobel too. They both deserved better than half measures. He also wanted to be careful about keeping his word, especially with things still unsettled between him and Isobel. He had hope...but not certainty. "I'm not leaving tomorrow, and I promise if I leave, I will talk to you first. I'm your forever friend."

"Cross your heart?" she asked with a hint of vulnerability.

"Cross my heart." He drew an X over his chest.

Smiling, the insecurity fading, she held up her arms for a hug. "I love you to the moon and back."

"Love you too, kiddo," he said, his heart in his throat as he leaned down to hug her in return, before dropping a kiss on top of her head.

This little girl had wrapped him around her finger from day one. He suspected she always would.

Easing back, she fanned a wave, placed her flowers in her lap, and rolled toward her friends playing horseshoes before the supper buffet.

From everything he'd heard about the day's event via Jacob, the response to the call for new registrants to the donor bank had been beyond expectations. He'd learned a lot about the process these past weeks and intended to keep pressing until Lottie had her match. Thank heaven she wasn't at the critical stage yet. They had time, even if they didn't know how much.

Once the child was safely in the children's play area, Cash pivoted toward the standing table where Isobel gathered with her sisters.

The sight of Isobel took his breath away. The evening's party was more formal than previous ranch gatherings. Isobel wore a tan flowy dress, her boots peeking just below the hem. Long feather earrings grazed her shoulders, tempting him to press his mouth the very same spot.

He worked to keep his eyes off the bandage on her forearm from where a branch had cut into her last night. She'd never made a sound. Had she worried he might pull her back up if she had? He couldn't guarantee otherwise.

* * *

Going to bed at two in the morning, he'd expected to be plagued by nightmares, but woke at first light to find he'd slept peacefully. Acknowledging his love for Isobel had eased something inside him. He didn't expect that the past would never torment him again. Although now he'd found a peace of sorts in what happened, a sense of having done his best. There was definitely something to be said for the healing found in Moonlight Ridge, whether it was mystical or the work of the O'Briens.

Straightening his bolero tie, he made his way across the party barn toward Isobel. The music and chatter muted in his ears as his focus narrowed to one woman. The only woman for him.

He rested a hand on Isobel's shoulder while addressing her sisters. "Do you mind if I steal this lovely lady away for a while? We're long overdue a conversation."

Neve pressed her lips tight. "That's for Isobel to decide."

"Of course." He hadn't mentioned his plans to her sisters, worrying they might give Isobel a heads-up. Although, given the playful light in Zelda's eyes, he suspected someone on the staff had spilled the beans. "Isobel, would you join me outside, where it's quieter?"

Private.

She looked up at him, her greenish-blue eyes sparkling reflections of the lights strung overhead. In her gaze, he saw the Isobel he'd come to know and treasure these past months. She was his friend—and his love.

Without hesitation, she slid her hand into his, holding firm. "I've been wanting to speak with you too."

Hope stirred at how quickly she'd agreed, although he reminded himself to be cautious. Her big heart would stop her from being impolite. Or she may simply want to tell him goodbye. He owed her an apology, but there was no guaranteeing she would accept.

Either way, he intended to do his level best to make things right again between them. And if she still told him to leave? His gut knotted at the thought. Glancing back at the band, he gave a quick nod to the lead singer, signaling the start of the request he'd discussed with them earlier.

As the first strains of "Always on my Mind" drifted through the sound system, Cash shouldered through the crowd and led her toward the barn's open double doors. The night sky beckoned with a full moon and a blanket of stars that shone brighter here in the mountains without the competing city halogens.

"That song," she said.

"From our dance." He clasped her hand tighter. "It's forever on my playlist."

He guided her the rest of the way to the side of the barn, where he'd set up a dining area, where the music could still be heard but they would have more privacy. Tiny lights were strung over their table for two, fresh flowers in the middle. A small dining cart waited off to the side with their food and a bottle of champagne. A little gift bag was perched in front of the ice bucket, with a Gems by River Jack gold sticker.

"Is this for us?" she asked hesitantly, then when he

nodded, she gasped and continued, "How did you find time to arrange everything today?"

"With help from our Top Dog friends." He hoped he was granted the honor of doing even more for Isobel for the rest of their lives. "Jacob and Hollie have created quite the community here."

Her face lit with smile. "Gran would approve of this…and the people of Moonlight Ridge."

Still standing, their fingers linked, he asked, "Are you okay that we haven't located her son yet for Lottie? And to return Gran's ring?"

"We made an incredible start these past weeks, and today as well." She pressed her palm to her heart. "I can't believe how far some people drove, agreeing to enter the donor base and register with Ancestry.com. I do think Gran's pregnancy must have been Moonlight Ridge's best kept secret ever."

"I'm sure she's smiling down on you proudly. The way you saved Sebastian last night was—" *terrifying* "—unbelievable."

"And you were a big part of that rescue. Not just with the way you kept me safe but also how you wove that story to distract Sebastian was inspired—inspired by Grandma Alice, that is."

"I learned the art of storytelling from the best— from you." He skimmed a lock of her hair from her face, excited to share the next part of his plan. "After same serious soul searching, I've also learned what's really important. I'm staying in Moonlight Ridge for the rest of the summer."

Hopefully longer, because he *wanted* to stay here, to

build a future in this special community full of people who understood the value of family and lifting each other up. But bottom line, Isobel and Lottie were his home.

"You're staying here? For the whole summer?" Her words tumbled out one on top of the other. Her eyes widened with shock and a hint of disbelief. "What about your new job?"

"I've already contacted them that I won't be accepting their offer after all." The call had been easier to make than he'd expected, like a weight had been lifted from his shoulders once he didn't have to say goodbye. "I'll go back to a fire department job someday, even here in Moonlight Ridge. But right now, I want to be here for you and Lottie."

"That would be…" Her voice quavered as she blinked back the sheen of tears. She cleared her throat and continued, "But I can't ask you to put your life on hold like that for us. There's so much unknown for me with Lottie's transplant surgery, although Dr. Barnett seems hopeful after today's event. Still, I'm not even sure when—or if—that will happen."

"You don't have to ask." He cupped her shoulders, aching to pull her close, but there was still more they needed to settle between them. With their entire future in the balance, he had to get this right.

He drew in a bracing breath, letting his thumbs stroke along the creamy softness of her neck. "If you're worried about me being gainfully employed, I have a workman's comp settlement from the accident that will tide me over. I also spoke with Jacob and Troy about one of the summer jobs listed on the ranch's website.

It's not glamorous work, but I'm wondering if some more time to decompress with the horses might be in order while I figure out my next step."

"You've really thought this through," she said, her voice full of cautious amazement.

"Yes, I have." Now came the most important part of his speech he'd been rehearsing all day as he'd prepared for this moment. "Thanks to you, I've discovered how to live again. And most importantly, how to love with my whole heart."

Gasping, she started to speak, but he pressed his fingers to her lips, needing to spell it all out. And if she returned his feelings? He still wanted to be the one to share his first. He only wished he'd sorted through them sooner.

"I love everything about you, Isobel. Seeing your brilliantly creative mind at work. Witnessing firsthand your compassion for others." So many images of Isobel spun through his mind in a beautiful kaleidoscope of memories. "Your drive and determination. The way you advocate for your amazing daughter—who has also utterly stolen my heart. Isobel, you are the most incredible person I've ever met."

She flattened her hands to his chest, speechless, her fingers curling into his lapels as if to anchor them both in the moment.

Baring his soul to her, he continued, "I'm not the best bargain, with all my scars—inside and out—but you and Lottie have become my world these past months. I was a fool to think I could leave. I want to dedicate my life to being the man you both deserve." He paused to take a breath, his pulse speeding at the possibility he may have misread her feelings. "If you need for us to go back to being friends for—"

This time, she pressed her fingers to his mouth, silencing him. "Cash, I have loved you since I saw you dressed as a pirate sipping tea with Lottie. You are every fantasy I ever dreamed of, and some I didn't even know were possible. You are a man of strength and honor." A slow, seductive smile curved her lips. "And you also make my toes curl when you kiss me."

Relief rolled over him, and he squeezed his eyes closed for a moment. He'd hoped for this answer, prayed, but he'd also feared being too late. Now a joy greater than any he'd known filled the empty corners of his soul.

He opened his eyes to Isobel, to their future.

"When I kiss you like this?" he said, grazing her mouth with his. "And this." He kissed her again, deeper, sealing their love and promises, fire coursing through his veins over the unbelievable gift of a lifetime of loving Isobel.

Which reminded him of one last detail.

Easing apart, he reached behind him to snag the gift bag from beside the chilling champagne. Her gaze followed his every move, her well-kissed mouth parting to whisper, "Oh my."

His heart slugging against his ribs, he dropped to one knee and pulled out the velvet ring box. "Isobel, love of my life, will you marry me?"

He creaked open the lid to reveal a diamond in a vintage setting with platinum scrollwork. "This ring was created here in Moonlight Ridge. It's a Gems by River Jack original, one of a kind, like you."

Her eyes filled with happy tears as she nodded. "Yes," she whispered, then louder, "yes, yes, of course I'll marry you. Build a life and family with you here in Moonlight Ridge."

She extended her hand for him to slide the ring in place, the stone refracting the moonlight in a prism of promises. This mountain sure had a way of delivering on happiness. He would be forever thankful to her grandmother, whose mission had brought them closer.

He linked their fingers together, pulling her close, the flowering scent of her hair mingling with the lush summer breeze. "May I have this dance?"

Sliding her arms up over his shoulders, pressing her soft curves against him. "Thanks to you, my dance card is officially full, now and forever."

Epilogue

Cocoa the Caring Canine Hears Wedding Bells

Love is in the air—and we all know I've got a top-notch sniffer!

Break out some extra milk bones. It's time to celebrate.

Lottie's mom is marrying her firefighter best friend. Cash gave Isobel the most beautiful ring at last week's summer festival held at the Top Dog Dude Ranch. The ring is a signature piece designed by Moonlight Ridge's very own Gems by River Jack.

It'll be a while before Isobel and Cash tie the knot, but I have it on good authority that plans are underway. Here's a sneak peek:

Her sisters will be bridesmaids.

Lottie's going to be a flower girl.

And—drum roll—I'll be the ring bearer. It's no secret that I love a job, and carrying that little pillow will be the most important work of the day.

Now that's what I call a fairy-tail ending. Isobel and her sisters just wish their grandmother was still alive to see the joy she'd made possible.

I never had the honor of meeting Gran, but I'm certain she is proud of how her granddaughters have embraced life at the Top Dog Dude Ranch. I know this because I can hear her approval whispering through the mountain pass.

In fact, Isobel tells me this whole adventure has inspired her to write a book about the history of Moonlight Ridge. She's learned a lot about legends and determined settlers in her search for her grandmother's long-lost relative.

Speaking of that search, the fantastic turnout at the Top Dog Dude Ranch's summer festival sure paid off. Lottie has five potential kidney donors. I'm not allowed to say who they are because of HIPAA laws. (Bet you didn't realize dogs understood privacy regulations.)

Let's just say, we don't know for sure yet if any of those five individuals is actually related to Lottie somehow, but I'm starting to figure it out. I have a hunch that things will turn out just right for both Gran and Lottie. So stay tuned for updates.

Life has turned out even better than I could have hoped for when we piled into the minivan back in Montana, bound for magical Moonlight Ridge. But when you partner a dog with enchantment?

The sky's the limit.

* * * * *